VITAMINS IN
CANCER PREVENTION
AND TREATMENT

VITAMINS IN CANCER PREVENTION AND TREATMENT

A Practical Guide

KEDAR N. PRASAD, PH.D.

Healing Arts Press
Rochester, Vermont

Healing Arts Press
One Park Street
Rochester, Vermont 05767

Note to the reader: This book is intended as an informational guide. The remedies, approaches, and techniques described herein are meant to supplement, and not to be a substitute for, professional medical care or treatment. They should not be used to treat a serious ailment without prior consultation with a qualified healthcare professional.

Prasad, Kedar N.
    Vitamins in cancer prevention and treatment : a practical guide / Kedar N. Prasad.
        p. cm.
    Published in 1989, this is a revised and updated edition of: Vitamins against cancer.
    Includes bibliographical references and index.
    ISBN 0-89281-483-7
    1. Cancer—Diet therapy. 2. Vitamin therapy. 3. Cancer—Nutritional aspects. 4. Cancer—Chemoprevention. I. Prasad, Kedar N. Vitamins against cancer. II. Title.
    RC271.V58P73   1993
    616.99'40654—dc20   93-20960
                                                             CIP

Printed and bound in the United States.

10 9 8 7 6 5 4 3 2

Text design by Virginia L. Scott

Healing Arts Press is a division of Inner Traditions International

Distributed to the book trade in Canada by Publishers Group West (PGW), Montreal West, Quebec

Distributed to the health food trade in Canada by Alive Books, Toronto and Vancouver

Distributed to the book trade in the United Kingdom by Deep Books, London

Distributed to the book trade in Australia by Millennium Books, Newtown, N. S. W.

Distributed to the book trade in New Zealand by Tandem Press, Auckland, New Zealand

Contents

Publisher's Note

The information presented in this book is offered for practical application by physicians and members of other recognized health professions. It may also be of personal value to those interested in preventing or treating cancer and its related effects. However, persons who believe they are suffering from serious illness should first consult a physician of their choice for diagnosis and care; the information in this book cannot be substituted for a medical treatment plan.

The findings published herein have resulted from numerous scientific studies; however, these do not represent the views of the university or associations with which the author is associated. While every effort has been made to provide the reader with reliable and current data, neither the publisher nor the author can assume responsibility for consequences from the application of this information.

Foreword

The lay public has become increasingly interested in monitoring personal health and has been besieged with recommendations from many different organizations and individuals. A particularly controversial area has been that of vitamins and cancer. Dr. Prasad has prepared a useful and well-organized antidote to the mass of irresponsible information about vitamins. He opens with a short, clever review of what is "fact and fiction" about vitamins and cancer; this perspective alone is worth the purchase of the book.

The author then presents in logical fashion the potential role of vitamins in the prevention and treatment of human cancer. His review of laboratory and epidemiological evidence for vitamins as natural inhibitors of cancer is well presented and understandable to the average individual. His interim guidelines for vitamin usage, diet changes, and lifestyle considerations for the prevention of human cancer are considered and reasonable. The distinction between the doses of vitamins and nutrients that may be necessary for adequate nutrition versus cancer prevention is an important issue and one that he presents in a balanced fashion.

Major new areas of research on the potential role of vitamins in the treatment of cancer or in alleviating the effects of treatment for cancer are discussed. The author's presentation of this rapidly developing field is well balanced, and research results are viewed with cautious optimism.

Finally, the list of more than one hundred internationally recognized clinical and laboratory investigators in the area of vitamins, nutrition, and cancer is extremely valuable and one that we hope will be used by the public.

As a physician who frequently sees bad results from the misuse of vitamins for nutrition or prevention or treatment of human cancer, I applaud Dr. Prasad for providing the public with a responsible presentation.

Frank L. Meyskens, Jr., M.D.
Director, University of California Cancer Center

Preface

An increasing number of people interested in improving and maintaining their health are using supplementary nutrition to achieve their goals. Recent studies estimate that about 40 percent of the people in the United States use some form of supplementary nutrition every day. Most of them are unaware of recent developments concerning nutrition and cancer, and many may be taking nutrients without using up-to-date scientific guidelines. The fact that excessive consumption of certain nutrients can cause irreversible damage to the body is well known.

This book has two major purposes: (1) to make the public aware of the results of recent research on vitamins, nutrition, and cancer; and (2) to provide interim guidelines that can be used to develop individual dietary and supplementary nutritional programs for cancer prevention and treatment. Such programs must be developed in close consultation with physicians who are knowledgeable about nutrition and cancer. The cancer prevention program may be equally effective for maintaining good health. Also included are a list of major scientific publications on vitamins, nutrition, and cancer, and an international list of more than one hundred major institutions where vitamins and nutrition are being used in the prevention and treatment of cancer.

1

What is Fact & What is Fiction?

A BRIEF DISCUSSION

During the last decade, many popular magazines and books have described new advances in vitamin and nutrition research. Unfortunately, many of these reports have made unsubstantiated claims regarding the usefulness of nutrition for maintaining good health and preventing cancer. As a result, a number of misconceptions have arisen concerning the value of nutrition. Some beliefs commonly held by the general public are discussed below.

1. **Fiction:** The more vitamins and other supplementary nutrients you take, the better you will feel.

   Fact: This belief can be dangerous. Consumption of excessive amounts of certain nutrients may cause severe damage. For instance, taking large amounts of vitamin A (50,000 I. U.* or more per day over a long period of time) may cause liver toxicity, and excess selenium (500 micrograms or more per day over a long period of time) may cause cataracts (an eye disease in which the lens becomes opaque).

2. **Fiction:** All the different forms of vitamins A, C, or E are similar and produce similar effects.

   Fact: The above statement is untrue. For example, retinoic acid is more effective than retinol or retinylacetate on cancer cells. Alpha-tocopherol can act as an antioxidant, whereas alpha-tocopheryl acetate and alpha-tocopheryl succinate do not. Although there is only one form of vitamin C, it is commonly prepared in combination with several minerals. Vitamin C preparations containing iron, manganese, and copper may be harmful, because vitamin C in the presence of these metals and oxygen produces toxic substances. Vitamin C preparations containing sodium, magnesium, and calcium have no such effects.

3. **Fiction:** Frozen fruit juices and powdered cold drinks after being mixed with water maintain high levels of vitamin C when stored in a refrigerator.

   Fact: This statement is also untrue. Frozen fruit juices and powdered cold drinks may provide beneficial amounts of vitamin C when drunk immediately after preparation. However, when it is stored in a cold place, vitamin C in solution rapidly deteriorates, and after twenty-four hours more than 50 percent of its activity is lost.

4. **Fiction:** Some people believe that to maintain good health or prevent cancer, they can take all their vitamins once in

---

* I.U.= International Unit.

the morning with breakfast; others believe that taking vitamins once in a while, especially during cold weather, is enough.

Fact: These beliefs are incorrect. The frequency with which one should take vitamins depends upon their rate of degradation in the body. Taking vitamins A and E orally twice a day (morning and evening) is adequate; this is not the case with vitamin C. Vitamin C is degraded rapidly in the body (usually within two to four hours); thus it is recommended that vitamin C be consumed at least four times a day. In addition, for cancer prevention, the consumption of vitamins at the appropriate time, depending on one's diet, is very important. Taking supplementary vitamins once in a while has no real health value.

5. **Fiction:** Avoiding excessive meat consumption is not relevant to preventing cancer.

    Fact: Wrong. Excessive consumption of meat in Western countries has been linked with colon cancer. This is further supported by the fact that the incidence of colon cancer among Seventh Day Adventists, who are vegetarians, is also low.

6. **Fiction:** Supplementary nutrition is not necessary for cancer prevention.

    Fact: Results of recent studies on human beings are not sufficient to fully support or reject the above view. However, there are a number of animal studies that suggest that supplementary nutrition is essential in preventing cancer.

7. **Fiction:** A balanced diet is sufficient for optimal protection against cancer.

    Fact: The concept of a "balanced diet" is very general. A balanced diet alone may not be adequate for optimal protection against cancer, although it is certainly better than a junk food diet. Taking beta-carotene and vitamins A, C, and E at appropriate times is also important, such as when one consumes food that contains cancer-causing substances. Receiving the required levels of these vitamins at the appropriate times only through a balanced diet may not be possible or practical. For these reasons, supplementary nutrition is essential for maximal protection against cancer.

8. **Fiction:** Our environment and our food and water are already polluted, and none of us can do anything about it. Therefore, we have to accept the increasing risk of cancer as a reality.

   Fact: Even though we cannot do very much immediately to remove cancer-causing substances from our environment and diet, we can certainly reduce their cancer-causing actions through proper food, supplementary nutrition, and lifestyle.

9. **Fiction:** An excess of zinc is necessary for maximal health and cancer prevention.

   Fact: This may not be true. Actually, excess zinc may block the action of selenium, an important anticancer agent.

10. **Fiction:** Cancer is a disease of old people, so you don't have to worry about a child's nutrition as a preventive measure.

    Fact: This may be true for some cancers, such as colon and rectal cancer. However, most cancers can occur at any age. Thus, for preventing cancer, proper nutrition is equally important for children.

11. **Fiction:** There is no scientific proof that supplementary vitamins are any good.

    Fact: The effectiveness of supplementary vitamins in preventing cancer and maintaining sound health has not been fully established in human beings. Forty to fifty years are needed before conclusive results become available. However, laboratory studies suggest vitamins can strengthen the body's immune defense system, reduce levels of cancer-causing substances, protect vital organs against the injurious effects of free radicals (harmful chemicals), block the action of cancer-causing substances, and suppress the growth of some kinds of cancer. Some of these benefits of vitamins have also been scientifically demonstrated in human beings.

12. **Fiction:** Most supplementary vitamins pass out of the body in the urine and feces, so why take them?

Fact: At this time we do not know what dose of vitamins is needed for maximum cancer prevention and maintaining sound health. The dietary vitamin E is present as mixed tocopherols which act as antioxidants, but they are unstable. The commercially made alpha-tocopheryl acetate is stable, but it does not act as an antioxidant until converted to alpha-tocopherol in the body. The turnover rate of vitamin C in the body is fairly rapid, so taking vitamin C in foods frequently enough to maintain sustained high levels in the body is not practical. Some excess amounts of vitamin C and vitamin E (alpha-tocopherol) are needed in the stomach to reduce levels of nitrosamines, potent cancer-causing agents, if nitrite-containing foods such as bacon, sausage, hot dogs and cured meats are eaten. The presence of these vitamins is necessary at the time such foods are consumed. Since we do not know the quantities of vitamins needed by the cells, giving them the opportunity to pick up the amounts they need is important. Thus, even though significant amounts of supplementary vitamins are excreted in the feces and urine, they may have already performed an important role in the body by then. For this reason, excess amounts of vitamins in the feces and urine should not be considered wasteful.

13. **Fiction:** Supplementary vitamin C causes kidney stones.

Fact: This effect has not been observed in normal adults. It is a well-established fact that if the urine becomes acidic, some of the waste products in the kidney may solidify and form "stones." However, this biological phenomenon usually occurs if there is an imbalance in body chemistry such that acidic solutions cannot be neutralized. The body normally has a tremendous capacity to neutralize any acidic solution that it takes in. In certain specific disease conditions in which one's body has lost this capacity, one should not take vitamin C in large amounts.

14. **Fiction:** Supplementary vitamins are addictive.

   Fact: Although high doses of vitamin C (up to 20 grams per day) have been used in treating heroin addiction, they have not caused permanent addictive changes in the body. However, persons who are taking high doses of supplementary vitamins should not stop abruptly. Because body systems may have adjusted to high doses of vitamins, sudden withdrawal may cause symptoms of vitamin deficiency.

15. **Fiction:** Vitamins and nutrients alone are sufficient to treat all cancers.

   Fact: Because of the complexities of cancer, neither vitamins nor any other agents can cure advanced tumors by themselves, but vitamins may be very useful in combination with other kinds of therapy. Vitamins may also help delay or prevent the recurrence of cancer. Using vitamins to treat cancer must be done according to scientific rationale; to use them otherwise may be ineffective.

16. **Fiction:** Beta-carotene acts only as a provitamin A, and has no function of its own.

   Fact: In addition to acting as provitamin A, beta-carotene produces some biological effects which are not caused by vitamin A.

17. **Fiction:** All types of vitamin E have the same effect on cancer cells.

Fact: Several experimental results show that alpha-tocopheryl succinate is the most effective form of vitamin E.

At this time, beta-carotene and vitamins A, C, and E are used as experimental agents, either alone or in combination in cancer prevention trials. In addition, they are used alone or in combination with conventional cancer treatment methods. The results of some of these studies are being published. Meanwhile, until better methods of cancer treatment are established, the utilization of all current treatment methods must be continued.

2

Preventing Cancer

WHAT CAUSES CANCER?

What are cancer cells?
Cancer cells divide like some normal cells, but unlike normal cells they continue to divide without any restriction and invade distant organs in the body. When normal cells are grown outside the body in laboratory petri dishes, a procedure known as tissue culture,* they have a limited lifespan, and all of them eventually die even when they have nutrients and space. In this

---

* Tissue culture is a method by which cells are grown in laboratory dishes containing adequate nutrients. This method is commonly used in cancer research because it is simple, sensitive, cost-effective, and efficient.

sense normal cells can be considered "mortal," whereas cancer cells are "immortal." Cancer cells will continue to grow in petri dishes indefinitely, provided sufficient nutrients and space are available.

Cancer can arise in any organ containing dividing cells (e.g., bone marrow, skin, intestine, and testes) or having cells that normally do not divide but that will divide if properly stimulated (e.g., liver cells, glia cells in the brain).

Certain tumors occur primarily among children. These include neuroblastoma (in the abdominal cavity), Wilms' tumor (in the kidney), medulloblastoma (in the brain), retinoblastoma (in the eye), and some types of leukemia (blood cancer). On the other hand, colon and rectal cancers are found primarily in persons over fifty years of age. Most other cancers can occur at any age. Cancers not only affect human beings and other mammals but also occur in lower organisms such as reptiles, frogs, fish, snails, and clams.

How do normal cells become cancerous?

Now we believe that normal cells have numerous sets of genes referred to as *protooncogenes*. Each protooncogene is made up of a specific segment of DNA* and produces a specific protein for cell functions. When these protooncogenes are activated by cancer-causing agents, they are called oncogenes. The accumulation of products (proteins) of multiple oncogenes within normal cells may convert them to cancer cells. Normal cells also contain sets of genes that are called *antioncogenes* or *tumor suppressor genes*. The products (proteins) of antioncogenes prevent the action of oncogenes on normal cells. The loss of antioncogenes can increase the risk of cancer formation. Agents

---

* DNA (deoxyribonucleic acid) molecules, also referred to as genes, are present in all cells.

that can activate protooncogenes or cause loss of antioncogenes are called *tumor initiators*. High doses of tumor initiators by themselves can produce cancer; low doses of tumor initiators cannot cause cancer unless they are helped by other agents called *tumor promoters*. Even high doses of tumor promoters generally do not produce cancer, but with prolonged exposure they may also be carcinogenic.

Human beings are seldom exposed to high doses of tumor initiators or promoters, but they are frequently exposed to low doses of these cancer-causing substances. Subsequent cancer-initiated events may remain dormant for ten to thirty years or more, until further genetic changes occur, and can appear as cancer cells if helped by other initiators or tumor promoters. Laboratory experiments have shown that the combined influence of two initiators is more effective than the individual agents in producing cancer. Some commonly known tumor initiators and tumor promoters are listed in Table 1. Most of these are found in the environment and diet (see pages 20–23 for a detailed description).

TABLE 1: COMMONLY KNOWN TUMOR INITIATORS AND PROMOTERS

TUMOR INITIATORS

Nitrosamine	Tobacco smoke
7, 12-Dimethylbenz(a) anthracene (DMBA)	Polychlorinated biphenyl (PCB)
Benzopyrene	Diethylstilbestrol (DES)
Asbestos	Aflatoxin
Ultraviolet radiation	Polyvinyl chloride (PVC)
Pesticides (malathion, parathion, kepone, DDT)	Some chemotherapeutic agents
Ionizing radiation (X rays and gamma rays)	Tar

TUMOR PROMOTORS	
Saccharine	Extract of unburned tobacco
Excess fat	Tobacco smoke condensate
12-O-tetradecanoyl-phorbol-13-acetate	Surface active agents (sodium lauryl sulfate)
High temperatures (43°–45° C or 109.4°–111° F)	Iodoacetic acid
Certain hormones such as estrogen	Phenobarbital

What is the rate of cancer in the United States?

It is estimated that one of every four Americans will develop some form of cancer. Since the current population of the United States is about two hundred fifty million, the total number of people now alive in this country who will develop cancer is about sixty-three million. A current estimate is that approximately one million new cases of cancer are diagnosed every year, and approximately one-half million people die of cancer every year. After cardiovascular disease, cancer is the second most common cause of death in the United States. The World Health Organization (WHO) has estimated that about eight million new cases of cancer are detected in the world each year, and about five million people die of this disease every year. However, this is an underestimation because tumor records are not accurately maintained in many parts of the world.

How much do diet and other environmental factors contribute to the incidence of cancer?

More than 90 percent of all human cancers are induced by environmental factors; 30–40 percent of these in men, and 50–60 percent in women, are thought to result from diet alone. Most of these cancers can be prevented by choosing a suitable diet, by taking appropriate amounts of nutritional supplements, by altering one's lifestyle, and by reducing the consumption of dietary and environmental cancer-causing substances as much as possible. Table 2 shows the incidence of death associated with certain types of cancer.

TABLE 2: THE PERCENTAGE OF DEATHS FROM CANCER OF
DIFFERENT PARTS OF THE BODY DIFFERS
IN MEN AND WOMEN

CANCER SITE	MEN	WOMEN
	(% OF TOTAL CANCER DEATHS)	
Lung	34	16
Colon and rectum	12	15
Prostate	10	—
Breast	—	19
Female reproductive organs (ovary, uterus, and cervix)	—	11

The relationship of diet and lifestyle to cancer has been observed in many parts of the world. Some examples are given on the following pages.

JAPAN

A high incidence of stomach cancer has been associated with the consumption of spices and pickled food. The rate of stomach cancer is markedly reduced among those Japanese immigrants who adopt Western food habits; however, the incidence of stomach cancer remains high among Japanese immigrants to the United States who continue to follow Japanese dietary habits.

CHILE

The high incidence of stomach cancer in Chile appears to be associated with consumption of food and drinking water that contain relatively high levels of nitrate, a chemical that combines with other chemicals (amines) in the stomach to form nitrosamine, a highly potent cancer-causing substance.

ICELAND

The incidence of stomach cancer among Icelanders who consume large quantities of smoked fish and meat is much higher than among those who eat such food in smaller amounts.

INDIA

The high incidence of oral cancer in India is associated with chewing betel nuts containing several cancer-causing agents. The habit of holding dry tobacco leaves between the lip and gum is associated with a high incidence of lip cancer. The latter is not unique to India, but is common to all regions where people chew tobacco in the manner described above.

Colon cancer is virtually absent among the Punjabi people in northwest India, who eat a diet rich in cellulose, vegetables, fiber, and yogurt.

UNITED STATES

The incidence of stomach cancer has decreased recently because of changing dietary habits. The rate of colon and rectal cancer among Seventh Day Adventists, who eat a vegetarian diet, is much less than among those who eat meat. In addition, Mormons, who do not smoke or drink alcohol or large quantities of coffee, have a lower incidence of colon and rectal cancer.

CHINA

In one province of China, people have a very high incidence of esophageal cancer. The high incidence of this cancer appears to be related to the fact that the selenium (an anticancer nutrient) content of the soil is very low. The people of this region eat mostly pickled food and only small quantities of fruits and vegetables.

What happens when meat is cooked over charcoal?

During warm weather, broiling meat over charcoal is a popular practice; however, recent studies suggest that this practice may increase the risk of cancer. On the other hand, if it is done in moderation and with scientific rationale, the possibility of such risk may be markedly reduced. To understand this, let us examine what happens when meat is cooked over charcoal.

As the meat cooks, fats drip down onto the hot charcoal, generating smoke that contains polycyclic aromatic hydrocarbons, such as benzopyrene, a powerful cancer-causing agent. The cooking meat is immediately exposed to and absorbs this smoke. Thus, charcoal-broiled meat contains carcinogenic substances from the smoke and noncharcoal-broiled meat does not. The amount of polycyclic aromatic hydrocarbons increases if the fat content of the meat is high and if it is cooked under conditions that expose it to high levels of fat-generated smoke. The average charcoal-broiled steak contains about 8 micrograms of polycyclic aromatic hydrocarbons per kilogram of steak.

In order to reduce the levels of cancer-causing substances in charcoal-broiled meat, the fat should be removed as much as possible before cooking. In addition, the meat may be placed a little farther away from the charcoal during cooking so that at least part of the fat-generated smoke will dissipate into the air before it can reach the meat. Covering the grill with aluminum foil before placing meat on it will also prevent smoke contamination. The cook and others should avoid inhaling the smoke. The quality of the prepared meat will in no way be compromised by following these recommendations.

What goes on in your body when you smoke?
Many studies have implicated tobacco smoking as a major cause of lung cancer, and 90 percent of all lung cancer cases are estimated to be caused by cigarette smoking. Reports show that lung cancer accounts for 30 percent of all cancer deaths in the United States. A study published in 1993 shows that at the highest smoking levels studied, female smokers showed 82 times the lung-cancer risk of the non-smoking women, whereas male smokers showed only 23 times the risk of non-smoking men. The reasons for this marked difference in sensitivity to tobacco smoking between men and women are unknown. In addition, smoking tobacco can cause chronic emphysema, a serious noncancer disease, with severe effects on the functioning of the lungs. Cigarette smoke contains a high level of nitrosamine, a potent cancer-causing agent, and nitrosating gases, which help form additional nitrosamines in the lungs. Nitrosamines are easily dissolved in water and can thus be absorbed through the mouth as well as the lung and deposited in other organs. Smoking also increases the risk of developing cancer of the larynx, mouth, and esophagus, and acts as a contributing factor for cancer of the urinary bladder, cervix, kidney, and pancreas.

Some studies have reported that smoking decreases the tissue levels of vitamins C and E. Therefore, if a person must smoke, he or she may wish to take vitamin C and E supplements. The exact amounts of these vitamins needed to replace those lost through smoking are unknown. Daily intakes of supplementary vitamins and selenium as discussed on page 57 should be adequate.

Red blood cells of smokers are more susceptible to lipid peroxidation (membrane damage) than those of nonsmokers. Supplementation with vitamin E has been reported to reduce the level of lipid peroxidation produced by free radicals. Smoking also results in folic acid deficiency primarily affecting bronchial squamous epithelial cells (lung cells) that become abnormal (metaplastic). This abnormality (metaplasia) can lead to cancer. Supplementation with 10 milligrams of folate and 0.5 milligram of vitamin B_{12} helps to reduce bronchial squamous metaplasia (precancerous changes).

What is the risk of cancer among nonsmokers who are exposed to tobacco smoke?

Some human studies suggest that a significant increase in lung cancer risk occurs among nonsmoking spouses of smokers. This risk is about two times higher than that found among nonsmoking couples. The children of smoking parents (one or both partners) may have an increased risk of developing lung cancer. Therefore, nonsmokers should avoid surroundings with high levels of tobacco smoke. One is encouraged by noting that smoking is now prohibited in many public places around the United States.

Are heavy drinkers more likely to get cancer?

About two-thirds of American adults consume alcohol, and about 17 percent of these are considered heavy drinkers. The average yearly consumption of alcohol in the United States is about three gallons per person.

There are no data to suggest that moderate consumption of alcohol alone increases the risk of cancer. However, there have been some reports that frequent drinking of wine or beer prepared in certain regions of the world (outside the United States) is associated with an increased risk of cancer of the esophagus, colon, and rectum. This is possibly because of impurities in the wine or beer, which may be carcinogenic.

Among alcohol abusers (those who drink heavily daily or most of the days of the week), the risk of not only esophageal cancer, but also of cancer of the mouth, head and neck, lip, liver, stomach, colon, rectum, and lung is markedly increased. Excessive consumption of alcohol also enhances the cancer-causing effects of smoking. The combined effects of alcohol and smoking on cancer risk are about two-and-a-half times greater than those produced by alcohol or smoking alone.

Some have suggested that excessive consumption of alcohol may increase the risk of cancer in the following ways:

(a) Alcohol contains small amounts of cancer-causing impurities.

(b) Cancer-causing substances are present in our diet and environment, and they are also formed in the intestine. Alcohol increases their solubility and hence the degree to which they may be absorbed by the body. This in turn may increase the risk of cancer.

(c) Some agents do not act as cancer-causing substances until they are converted to an active form. Alcohol may facilitate the conversion.

(d) Alcohol suppresses the body's immune defense system.

(e) Alcohol may cause nutritional deficiencies, thereby increasing the risk of cancer. Excess alcohol may cause a deficiency in proteins; vitamins A, C, and E; folic acid; thiamine (B_1); pyridoxine (B_6); and certain minerals such as magnesium, zinc, iron, copper, and molybdenum. Deficiencies in vitamins A, C, and E may play an important role in increasing the risk of cancer induced by alcohol.

Thus, to reduce the risk of cancer of the upper intestinal tract, mouth, and lung, one should avoid excessive alcohol consumption. Those who consume moderate amounts of alcohol should not smoke at the same time, and should ensure through diet and nutritional supplements that body levels of vitamins A, C, and E do not decrease.

Does excessive coffee or tea consumption increase the risk of cancer?

Research has shown that caffeinated and decaffeinated coffee contain substances that at high concentrations are mutagenic.* These results suggest that substances other than caffeine are also responsible for changes in the genetic materials. Similarly, some indirect human studies also indicate that excessive consumption of either caffeinated or decaffeinated coffee is associated with an increased risk of bladder, pancreas, and stomach cancer; however, other studies have not confirmed these results. Readily oxidized phenolic compounds that are normally present in coffee may facilitate the formation of nitrosamine from nitrite and amines in the stomach. Thus, it appears that if large amounts of nitrosamines are formed in the stomach because of an excessive consumption of coffee, the risk of certain cancers, especially stomach and pancreas cancer, may be increased. Again, caffeine alone does not seem to be associated with an increased risk of cancer. This finding is further supported by the fact that animal studies have so far failed to show that caffeine by itself produces cancer.

A recent study from England has reported that heavy tea consumption increases the risk of cancer of the pancreas. The cancer-causing substances in the tea have not been identified. One of the factors could be caffeine.

Caffeine is known to cause genetic changes, as well as to reduce the capacity of cells to repair damage produced by agents such as radiation and chemicals. Therefore, excess caffeine may enhance the effect of cancer-causing substances so that it acts as a tumor promoter. Further studies are needed to define the role of excessive consumption of coffee, tea, and caffeine in the development of cancer in human beings.

---

* Alterations in genetic materials cause mutations that in most cases are not expressed. Examples of expressed mutations include hemophilia, color blindness, and Huntington's chorea. Substances that cause mutations are called mutagenic.

SOME ENVIRONMENTAL AGENTS KNOWN TO CAUSE CANCER

Ionizing Radiation (X Rays and Gamma Rays)

Ionizing radiation is commonly used to diagnose human diseases and to treat cancer. However, such radiation may also cause cancer.

The minimum dose (single and whole-body) needed to induce leukemia in adults is about 20 rad (radiation absorbed dose) (1 rad is equal to the radiation exposure of approximately thirty-three chest X-ray films). However, any amount of radiation may induce leukemia in human fetuses. Repeated exposure to smaller doses of radiation is more likely to produce leukemia than a large single dose. Most leukemias appear within ten years from the time of radiation exposure.

The minimum dose of radiation needed to produce breast cancer is about 1 rad. Breast tissue is more sensitive to radiation during pregnancy. The minimum time interval between exposure to radiation and cancer development is about five years, and the maximum time interval is about thirty years.

The minimum dose of radiation needed to produce thyroid cancer is about 7 rad. Women are approximately two times more sensitive than men, and Jewish women may be about seventeen times more sensitive than non-Jewish women. The reasons for these differences are unknown at this time. The time interval between exposure to radiation and cancer development may vary from ten years to over thirty-five years.

Doses commonly used in radiation therapy (a total of 3,000-4,000 rad, given at 200 rad/day, 1,000 rad/week) can induce cancer in most organs ten to thirty years after the completion of radiation therapy. This aspect is discussed in detail in chapter 3.

Since there is no radiation dose known to be "safe," continuous efforts must be made to minimize exposure as much as possible. The extent to which these efforts are successful may well affect the whole future of nuclear energy. No one should be exposed to any extra radiation unless it is necessary for his or her health. There is no reason why a person should not ask a physician or dentist if an X-ray examination is really necessary.

Some laboratory studies suggest that the combination of X-ray radiation and chemical carcinogens is nine times more likely to cause cancer than the individual agents alone. X-ray radiation also increases virus-induced cancer formation in laboratory experiments.

Ultraviolet (UV) Radiation

Exposure to UV radiation (part of the radiation from the sun; also called nonionizing radiation) is greater for people who reside at higher altitudes and in areas with high sun exposure. Skin cancers such as melanoma can result from exposure to UV radiation. White skin is more prone to develop melanoma than black; however, the progression of melanoma in persons with black skin is much more rapid than in those with white skin. The use of a sun screen (skin lotion) may reduce the effects of UV radiation during sunbathing. Some studies have reported that the combination of UV radiation and X-ray radiation is twelve times more likely to produce cancer cells than the individual agents. In addition, tumor promoters present in the diet and environment may also increase the risk of UV radiation-induced cancer formation and may be partly responsible for a five-fold increase in melanoma incidence in the sunbelt states of the United States. One should note that chemical carcinogens that increase the risk of X-ray induced cancer fail to increase the risk of UV radiation-induced cancer.

The time interval between exposure to UV radiation and the formation of detectable cancer is generally more than ten years.

Chemotherapeutic Agents

Most of the chemotherapeutic agents that are currently used in the treatment of cancer can also produce cancer in human beings. This takes about ten to thirty years before new cancer appears after chemotherapy.

Compounds

The following compounds and agents are carcinogenic:

Dioxin, a by-product of herbicide and pesticide production, is one of the most toxic substances produced by humans; exposure to only one part per billion is hazardous to human health.

Polyvinyl chloride (PVC), commonly found in packaging materials.

Pesticides, commonly found in meat and nonmeat foods.

Polychlorinated biphenyls (PCBs), commonly found in packaging materials and fish obtained from contaminated rivers.

Diethylstilbestrol (DES), a synthetic female hormone commonly fed to cattle.

Polycyclic aromatic hydrocarbons, commonly present in air pollution and charcoal-broiled meat.

Asbestos, commonly found in certain building materials such as roofing and water-pipe insulation.

Aflatoxin, a mold (fungus) found on peanuts and peanut butter if they are not well preserved.

Viruses

Certain viruses have been shown to increase the risk of cancer in human beings. For example, hepatitis B virus may increase the risk of liver cancer and viruses have been associated with some types of human lymphoma (blood cell tumor).

Table 3 describes some dietary and lifestyle factors that may be associated with specific cancer types.

TABLE 3: RELATIONSHIPS BETWEEN DIET, LIFESTYLE, AND CANCER RISK

PROBABLE CAUSATIVE AGENTS (DIET AND LIFESTYLE)	TYPE OF CANCER
Excess fat	Prostate, breast, stomach, colon, rectum, pancreas, and ovary
Excess protein	Breast, endometrium, prostate, colon, rectum, pancreas, and kidney
Excess total caloric intake	Most cancer, not related to any particular types
Excess alcohol	Esophagus, mouth, head and neck, lip, stomach, liver, colon, and rectum
Smoking	Lung, larynx, mouth, and esophagus
Excess alcohol plus smoking	Mouth, larynx, esophagus, and lung
Excess alcohol, smoking, and excess coffee	Pancreas, lung, liver, mouth, larynx, and esophagus
Excess coffee, tea	Bladder, pancreas, and stomach
Excess saccharine	Bladder
Cadmium from diet, smoking, and occupation	Kidney
Excess zinc	All cancers, especially breast and stomach
Iron deficiency	Stomach and esophagus
Iodine deficiency	Thyroid
Excess smoked meat or fish, excess charcoal-broiled meat, excess pickled products	Stomach
Certain viruses	Liver, certain blood cancers

Interpretation of Animal Data

In most animal studies, a single cancer-causing agent is tested to determine its carcinogenic potential. Animal studies are often criticized on the basis that high doses of a single carcinogen are needed to produce tumors. Some argue that since humans are not exposed to such high levels, the same carcinogen cannot produce cancer in humans. However, human beings are chronically exposed to multiple cancer-causing agents at very low doses. Recent experimental studies of animals have shown that a combination of two cancer-causing agents is more effective in producing cancer than the agents alone. These results suggest that the doses of carcinogens needed to produce cancer in human beings may be very low.

MAJOR WARNING SIGNALS FOR CANCER

General: Weakness and weight loss, fatigue.

Breast Cancer: Persistent lump, blood or blood-stained discharge from nipple, nonhealing ulcer.

Lung cancer: Persistent cough, coughing up blood, chest pain.

Cervical cancer: Spotting of blood after intercourse, painful coitus, foul discharge from vagina.

Skin cancer: Increase in size of mole, ulceration of mole, change in color of mole, pain at the site of mole, nonhealing and persistent ulcer.

Rectal and colon cancer: Alternate diarrhea and constipation, blood discharge in stool associated with weight loss.

Bone cancer: Prolonged pain in bone without any injury, with or without swelling.

Testicular cancer: Persistent firm to hard swelling in testis, usually without pain.

Hodgkin's Disease: Firm and painless enlargement of lymph
nodes, fever, excess sweating, fatique.
Leukemia: Weakness, loss of appetite, bone and joint pain,
fever, lymph node swelling.

HOW TO PROTECT AGAINST CANCER

We can reduce the risk of cancer in two ways. First, we can
attempt to eliminate as many cancer-causing agents (tumor
initiators and tumor promoters) from the environment and the
diet as possible. Second, we can reduce the effectiveness of
carcinogens by taking anticarcinogenic substances and having
an appropriate diet. The first approach appears simple, but in
reality it is the more difficult, since it requires legislation and
dramatic alterations in lifestyles and dietary habits. The second approach appears more practical and may be nearly as
effective. This approach involves reducing our intake of cancer-
causing substances by diet modification as much as possible
and increasing our use of specific dietary components by diet
modification and supplementation, which have been demonstrated to reduce the formation and effectiveness of cancer-
causing agents. The above approach also includes changing
lifestyle by complete cessation of smoking tobacco and chewing
tobacco products, and by following other guidelines described
on pages 55–58.

What are the known dietary anticancer agents?
Many laboratory experiments have shown that there are several agents in the diet that may reduce the risk of cancer caused
by radiation and a wide range of chemical carcinogens. These
specific anticancer nutrients include the following:

Vitamins

Beta-carotene and vitamins A, C, and E are potent anticancer agents that may reduce the risk of cancer in animals. Although analyses of dietary habits and cancer incidence have shown that these vitamins may also reduce the risk of cancer in human beings, conclusive proof is still lacking. This is primarily because experiments analogous to animal tumor studies have not been performed in human beings. In animals studies, the effect of a vitamin supplement on the incidence of cancer is evaluated; in human studies the effectiveness of a diet rich in beta-carotene and vitamins A, C, and E is generally evaluated, rather than the individual vitamins. Thus, comparing animal and human studies is difficult. Other vitamins such as vitamin B complex (except folic acid and riboflavin), vitamin D, and vitamin K do not appear to prevent cancer in animals or human beings, but they are necessary for many body functions. Some animal studies have shown that supplemental riboflavin reduces the risk of chemical-induced liver and skin cancer. Deficiency of riboflavin enhances the growth of chemical-induced skin cancer. The relevance of these observations for human cancer is unknown. Folic acid deficiency may cause premalignant changes in the human lung.

Protease Inhibitors

Protease inhibitors are found in larger amounts in soybeans. They inhibit the activities of cellular enzymes called proteases, which destroy proteins in cells. The precise balance between the rate of formation and destruction of protein is maintained in the cells for their optimal function. Protease inhibitors even at moderately high doses can disturb this balance and may produce toxic effects. Some laboratory experiments suggest that adding protease inhibitors, such as antipain, blocks cancer formation by X rays and also the action of tumor promoters. The significance of protease inhibitors in reducing the risk of cancer in human beings is being evaluated.

Minerals

Among minerals, selenium appears to be a very potent anticancer agent for animal tumors. An antioxidant enzyme, glutathione peroxidase, requires selenium in order to exert its antioxidant action. Selenium in combination with vitamin E is more effective than either of the individual agents alone. Analyses of dietary intake of selenium and cancer incidence have shown that it may also reduce the risk of cancer in human beings.

Other Dietary Factors

Among other dietary factors, fiber appears to be most important in reducing the risk of cancer, especially of colon and rectal cancer and possibly other tumors.

HOW VITAMINS CAN PREVENT CANCER

Beta-carotene and vitamins A, C, and E may reduce the incidence of cancer in multiple ways, some of which are described below:

Vitamins can act as antioxidants

Beta-carotene, vitamin A (retinol, retinoic acid, but not retinyl palmitate or retinyl acetate), vitamin E (alpha-tocopherol, but not alpha-tocopheryl acetate, alpha-tocopheryl succinate or alpha-tocopheryl nicotinate), and vitamin C (ascorbic acid, sodium ascorbate or calcium ascorbate) act as antioxidants; that is, they destroy free radicals. Free radicals are harmful molecules that form normally in the body. They have a free electron that makes them highly reactive and capable of damaging neighboring molecules such as DNA, RNA, protein, and lipid. Many cancer-causing agents damage normal cells by generating excessive amounts of free radicals. Thus, higher levels of these vitamins within or outside cells may protect them from the damaging effects of free radicals.

Vitamins can inhibit the formation of
cancer-causing substances

Vitamins C and E may prevent the formation and reduce the levels of certain cancer-causing substances in the intestinal tract. For example, nitrites are commonly used to preserve meat and are present in bacon, sausage, hot dogs, and cured meat. Nitrites by themselves do not cause cancer, but they can combine with amines in the stomach to form nitrosamines.

Nitrite + Amine = Nitrosamine

Nitrosamines are among the most potent cancer-causing agents for both animals and human beings. They are very soluble in water and therefore can be readily absorbed and distributed to all the tissues in the body. The presence of vitamin C or vitamin E (alpha-tocopherol) in the stomach may prevent the formation or reduce the levels of nitrosamines.

Nitrite + Amine + Vitamin C or Vitamin E =
Little or No Nitrosamine

Thus, taking vitamin C or vitamin E just before eating food containing nitrites may reduce or prevent the formation of nitrosamines in the stomach. The amount of vitamin C or vitamin E needed depends upon the amount of nitrites consumed. At this time, the precise amount of vitamin C or vitamin E needed to reduce the formation of nitrosamines cannot be determined. However, one can estimate that for an average meal containing nitrites, taking 200–250 milligrams of vitamin C and 50 I.U. of alpha-tocopherol immediately before eating may be adequate.

In addition to nitrosamines, many other mutagenic substances (agents that cause genetic changes that may or may not lead to cancer) are formed in the intestinal tract. Many mutations (changes in genetic materials) precede cancer formation. Studies have shown that the levels of mutagenic substances in the feces are higher for persons who are meat eaters than for those who are vegetarians. The presence of higher levels of fecal mutagenic substances may increase the risk of cancer. This hypothesis is supported by the fact that the incidence of cancer among Seventh Day Adventists, who are vegetarians, is much less than for people who eat meat. It has been reported that taking vitamin C or vitamin E reduces the levels of mutagenic substances in the feces of meat-eaters. Furthermore, reports indicate that taking both vitamins C and E is more effective than taking either individually. Estimating the amounts of vitamins needed is difficult; however, doses of 250 milligrams of vitamin C and 100 I.U. of alpha-tocopherol may be adequate to reduce the levels of mutagenic substances in the intestine.

In addition, many chemicals are not carcinogenic until they are converted to an active form in the body. In some cases vitamins A, C, and E can prevent the conversion of inactive forms of such cancer-causing substances to active forms.

Vitamins can reduce the action of cancer-causing agents

Many experimental studies suggest that beta-carotene and vitamins A, C, and E may inhibit the cancer-causing action of tumor promoters as well as tumor initiators. In order for such inhibition to occur, high levels of beta-carotene and vitamins A, C, and E must be maintained in the cells; the optimal doses are unknown. Recommended doses and dose schedules of vitamins for cancer prevention are described on page 57.

Recent advances in cancer research have identified several cancer risk factors at the molecular level resulting from structural, conformational, and functional changes in DNA. Some of them include: a) activation of protooncogenes, b) loss of antioncogenes, c) abnormal rearrangement of normal genes, and d) stimulation of cell-signaling systems. No single factor can cause cancer, but any one can trigger normal cells to become cancerous if they have already accumulated other cancer risk factors. Recent studies suggest that some vitamins can reduce the expression of one or more risk factors.

The expresson of c-*myc*, an oncogene, has been shown to increase in some mouse and human tumors *in vivo* and *in vitro*; however, this oncogene is also elevated during rapid growth of normal cells. Therefore, an elevation of the level of c-*myc* expression by itself may not be considered a cancer risk factor. However, it may become a cancer risk factor when the cells have already accumulated other cancer risk factors. Vitamin A (retinoic acid, a metabolite of vitamin A) vitamin D (1 $\propto$ -25 $(OH)_2D_3$), and vitamin E (alpha-tocopheryl succinate) reduce the expression of c-*myc* in some cancer cells *in vitro*.

The increased expression of H-*ras* oncogene is also considered a cancer risk factor. Vitamins A and E reduce the expression of H-*ras* in some tumor cells *in vitro*. The effect of these vitamins on the expressions of c-*myc* and H-*ras* in normally dividing cells has not been evaluated. However, high doses of vitamins A, E, or C do not affect the proliferation of normal cells. This is because normally dividing cells discriminate against the uptake of excessive anounts of these vitamins. When these cells become abnormal because of accumulation of multiple genetic damages, they lose the ability to discriminate against excessive intake of vitamins. Therefore, the reduction in the expression of c-*myc* and H-*ras* oncogenes by vitamins can occur in either cancerous or precancerous cells but not in normal ones. Additional studies are needed to substantiate these observations in humans.

An increased proliferation of epithelial cells in the colon is considered a risk factor for developing colon cancer. A recent study has reported that supplementation with vitamins A, C, and E reduces this abnormality in human colon cells.

Vitamins can change newly formed
or established cancer cells back to normal cells

Some recent laboratory experiments suggest that vitamins A, C, and E may convert newly formed or well-established cancer cells to normal cells. For example, vitamin C has been shown to reverse new chemically induced cancer cells to normal cells. Vitamin C does not have this effect on well-established cancer cells. However, vitamin A has been shown to transform some well established cancer cells to cells resembling normal cells. Some tumors such as lung cancer, prostate cancer, colon cancer, and neuroblastoma (a tumor of embryonic nerve cells) respond to vitamin A in the above manner. Similarly, alpha-tocopheryl succinate, a form of vitamin E, also transforms some established cancer cells such as melanoma (a form of skin cancer) to normal cells in mice. It also permanently stops the growth of some other tumor cells such as glioma tumor, prostate carcinoma, neuroblastoma, and leukemia cells. Recent laboratory experiments show that alpha-tocopheryl succinate is more potent than other forms of vitamin E (e.g., alpha-tocopheryl acetate, alpha-tocopheryl nicotinate and alpha-tocopherol) in reducing the growth of cancer cells and enabling them to become more like normal cells. A recent study suggests that alpha-tocopheryl succinate acts as a more effective antioxidant *in vitro* than alpha-tocopherol. Beta-carotene can also convert some cancer cells to cells that are more like normal cells. Beta-carotene and alpha-tocopheryl succinate also enhance the effectiveness of other agents that are known to convert cancer cells to cells that are more like normal cells.

The exact amounts of vitamins needed to reverse cancerous or precancerous cells to normal cells are not known for human beings; however, the doses and dose schedules described on page 57 may be adequate for this mechanism.

Vitamins can stimulate
the body's immune defense system against cancer

Beta-carotene and vitamins A, C, and E have been shown to stimulate the body's defense system, which in turn may kill newly formed cancer cells, or the remaining few established cancer cells, in patients who are in a state of remission. The amounts needed to achieve these effects are unknown. However, some studies have shown that vitamin C (up to 4 grams orally per day), vitamin E alpha-tocopherol (1,200 I.U. orally per day), and vitamin A (12,000 I.U. orally per day) stimulate the human body's immune defense system. In preliminary studies, beta-carotene supplementation improves the immune system of patients with advanced AIDS. These studies were performed in patients who were also taking AZT, an immunosuppressive drug. In order to evaluate the efficiency of beta-carotene accurately, the above study should also be performed in the absence of AZT. In addition, the combined effect of beta-carotene and vitamins A, C, and E on the immune system of patients with AIDS should be evaluated.

The vitamin mechanisms described above are relevant to cancer prevention. These mechanisms of action of vitamins are now being studied in human beings by epidemiological methods and by intervention trials with supplemental vitamins. Several epidemiological studies in humans have shown that diets rich in beta-carotene, vitamin E, and vitamin C reduce the risk of cancer. However, some studies have failed to confirm the above results. This inconsistency in results is due to the fact that there are numerous inherent problems associated with the use of epidemiological methods in the study of vitamins and cancer. For instance, the plasma levels of vitamins in some cases may not reflect tissue levels. To demonstrate the involvement of vitamins in the prevention of human cancer, we must show in an intervention trial that an increased intake of supplementary beta-carotene, vitamin A, vitamin C, vitamin E, or all four, reduces the risk of cancer among high-risk human populations. Some high-risk populations are smokers (lung cancer), asbestos workers (lung cancer), and persons with polyps (colon cancer). Only such human studies can be considered analogous to animal experiments in which increased amounts of supplemental vitamins in the diet have reduced the risk of chemically induced tumors. Several such human studies are currently in progress, and others are being planned. Beta-carotene and vitamin E have been shown to reverse precancerous lesions, most notably oral leukoplakia. The results of a large intervention trial in China, published in 1993, revealed that supplementation with multiple vitamins and minerals reduced cancer incidence by 13 percent and overall death by 9 percent. A definitive answer regarding the role of beta-carotene and vitamins A, C, and E in the prevention of human cancer will come from these studies, but it will be many, many years before complete data become available. Thus, the interim dietary, lifestyle, and supplementary nutrition guidelines described in this book should be considered tentative and open to revision as new scientific results on human beings become available. (When estimating doses of vitamins to be taken on a regular basis, one must also be aware of dose ranges within which these vitamins do not produce any toxic effects in human beings.)

Most of the above descriptions of vitamin mechanisms of action are based on animal and cell culture studies. These studies are often criticized, because the results may not be applicable to human cancers. However, these new ideas and concepts can only be developed by these experimental models in a cost- and time-effective manner. In addition, many studies on cancer-protective agents use chemical carcinogens or radiation in order to evaluate their protective effects. Such studies involving carcinogens cannot be performed on humans. In order to test the hypothesis developed on animal and cell culture models in humans, a similar experimental design must be used.

For example, the cancer preventive role of vitamins in animals has been demonstrated by using supplemental vitamins. The same action of vitamins, however, cannot be demonstrated in human epidemiological studies in which *no* supplemental vitamins are given. This may be one of the reasons why the results of human epidemiological studies on vitamins and cancer have not been consistent. The mechanistic studies of vitamin action can only be performed on cell culture systems.

VITAMIN NUTRITION

What are some rich dietary sources of vitamins?

Beta-carotene

Vegetables: Beet greens, broccoli, carrots, pumpkins, spinach, sweet potatoes, cabbage, lettuce, yellow corn

Fruits: Cantaloupe, apricots, mangoes

Animal Products: Liver, eggs, milk

Vitamin A

Liver, eggs, and milk are excellent sources.

Vitamin C

Vegetables: Brussels sprouts, cauliflower, peas, cabbage, green peppers

Fruits: Oranges, lemons, limes, pineapples, raspberries, strawberries, grapefruit

Vitamin E

Vegetable oils, nuts, and whole grains are the richest sources of vitamin E; vegetables, fruits and animal products contain small amounts.

Vegetables: Spinach, parsley, mustard greens, turnip leaves, asparagus

Fruits: Apple skins, tomatoes, cucumbers, bananas

Animal Products: Fish, chicken, steak

WHAT FORMS OF VITAMINS ARE AVAILABLE?

Beta-carotene

Forms: Beta-carotene is one of six hundred carotenoids found in fruits and vegetables. Beta-carotene is commercially available and is commonly used.

In Blood: Primarily beta-carotene and other carotenoids.

In Tissues: Stored primarily in the fatty tissue of skin. Beta-carotene is converted to retinol in the wall of the intestine by an enzymatic reaction. One molecule of beta-carotene produces two molecules of retinol. In humans, the above conversion of beta-carotene does not occur if the body has sufficient amounts of retinol.

Solubility: Soluble in lipids and alcohol.

Beta-carotene can be taken in soft gelatin. In addition, other carotinoids should be taken by consuming fruits and vegatables.

Vitamin A

Forms: Retinyl acetate, retinol and retinyl palmitate are available. Retinyl acetate is converted to retinol in both the lumen and the wall of the intestine. Retinol is oxidized to retinoic acid in cells.

In Blood: Primarily retinol.

In Tissues: Primarily retinoic acid; stored in the liver as retinyl palmitate.

Solubility: Soluble in lipids and alcohol, but not in water.

Vitamin A can be taken as retinyl acetate or retinyl palmitate. Laboratory experiments suggest that solvents of some vitamin A preparations (water soluble) are very toxic. Thus, the use of such solvents should be avoided. A vitamin A preparation in a gelatin capsule containing water and glycerine or oil may be recommended.

Vitamin C

Forms: Vitamin C is sold commercially as ascorbic acid, sodium ascorbate (1 gram of vitamin C contains 124 milligrams of sodium), sodium ascorbate—minimum sodium (1 gram of vitamin C contains 62 milligrams of sodium), calcium ascorbate, timed-release capsules containing ascorbic acid, and capsules containing ascorbic acid and certain minerals.

In Blood and Tissues: Primarily ascorbic acid.

Solubility: Both sodium ascorbate and calcium ascorbate are easily dissolved in water.

If one has no signs of hypertension or hyperacidity in the stomach, sodium ascorbate with minimum sodium is acceptable. If hypertension is present, ascorbic acid or calcium ascorbate may be recommended. If hyperacidity is present, sodium ascorbate or calcium ascorbate may be recommended.

Vitamin E

Forms: Synthetic forms are referred to as dl-forms; natural forms are referred to as d-forms. The common commercial form of vitamin E is d- or dl-alpha-tocopherol. Other forms of vitamin E are d- or dl-alpha-tocopheryl acetate, alpha-tocopheryl succinate, and alpha-tocopheryl nicotinate. These forms of vitamin E are converted to alpha-tocopherol in the lumen and wall of the intestine. A recent study shows that a portion of alpha-tocopheryl succinate can enter the blood during supplementation with 800 I.U. of alpha-tocopheryl succinate.

In Blood and Tissues: Primarily alpha-tocopherol.

Solubility: Soluble in lipids and alcohol, but not in water.

Laboratory experiments have shown that the solvents of some vitamin E preparations (water soluble) are toxic. Therefore, the use of such solvents should be avoided. A vitamin E preparation in a gelatin capsule containing water and glycerine or oil is recommended. Vitamin E should be taken both as alpha-tocopherol and alpha-tocopheryl succinate, since the latter has been found to be the most effective form of vitamin E in experimental systems.

HOW TO STORE VITAMINS

Beta-carotene

Beta-carotene can be stored at room temperature, away from light, for several months.

Vitamin A

Crystal forms of retinol and retinoic acid may be stored in the cold, away from light, for several months. Other forms of vitamin A can also be stored at room temperature for several months.

Vitamin C

Vitamin C should not be stored in solution form because it is easily destroyed. Crystal or tablet forms of vitamin C can be stored at room temperature, away from light, for several months.

Vitamin E

Alpha-tocopherol, alpha-tocopheryl acetate, and alpha-tocopheryl succinate can be stored at room temperature, away from light, for several months.

CAN VITAMINS BE DESTROYED DURING STORAGE?

Beta-carotene

Beta-carotene crystals or solutions are rapidly destroyed when exposed to light.

Vitamin A

No form of vitamin A in solution will degrade significantly at room temperature, away from light, at least for several months. However, retinoic acid and retinol (solution or powder) are rapidly destroyed when they are exposed to light. Domestic cooking does not destroy retinol and beta-carotene, but slow heating over a long period of time may reduce their potency. Canning and prolonged cold storage may also reduce vitamin A activity. The vitamin A content of fortified milk powder substantially decreases after two years.

Vitamin C

Vitamin C in solution is destroyed by light, heat, and air. Freezing, thawing, and cold storage of solutions of vitamin C reduce its potency. Vitamin C solutions in the presence of air and copper, iron, or manganese generate free radicals (harmful chemical species). Thus, the mixing of vitamin C with any of these minerals should be avoided.

Vitamin E

Alpha-tocopherol in solution is easily destroyed, whereas alpha-tocopheryl acetate and alpha-tocopheryl succinate solutions are not. Destruction of vitamin E increases in the presence of light, oxygen, and trace metals such as iron and copper. Food processing, frying, freezing, and drying quickly destroy vitamin E. The vitamin E content of fortified milk powder is unaffected over a two-year period.

WHY WE NEED VITAMIN SUPPLEMENTS

Does the human body make its own vitamins?

Human beings do not make their own beta-carotene or vitamins A, C, and E. We depend on fresh fruits, vegetables, fish, meat, and dairy products, as well as vitamin supplements, for these essential nutrients.

Beta-carotene—primarily from fresh fruits and vegetables.

Vitamin A—primarily from meats, eggs, and milk.

Vitamin C—primarily from fresh fruits and vegetables.

Vitamin E—primarily from vegetable oil.

When we take vitamins, how much does the body absorb?

Beta-carotene

Only about 10 percent of ingested beta-carotene is absorbed from the small intestine. Among vegetarians, most of beta-carotene is converted to retinol, whereas among nonvegetarians who have sufficient amounts of vitamin A, the above conversion does not occur. The turnover of beta-carotene in blood is slow; therefore, it can be taken once a day.

Vitamin A

Only about 10–20 percent of ingested vitamin A is absorbed from the small intestine. Normal cells characteristically do not pick up more than they need to function. Liver cells are an exception. Retinyl acetate is converted to retinol in the wall of the intestine. Retinol is further converted to retinoic acid in cells; however, most of the body's vitamin A is stored in the liver as retinyl palmitate.

Since the maximum level of retinol in blood appears three to six hours after ingestion of vitamin A and drops to a basal level in about ten to twelve hours, it should be taken twice a day (once in the morning and once in the evening) to maintain higher levels.

Vitamin C

The amount of absorption of ingested vitamin C varies from 20–80 percent, depending upon the dose. If one consumes 200–500 milligrams, only 50 percent (100–250 milligrams) will be absorbed from the intestine. If one takes more than the above doses, absorption of vitamin C is further reduced. On this basis, one should not take more than 500 milligrams per dose. In order to reduce the formation of cancer-causing substances in the stomach and intestine, certain amounts of unabsorbed vitamin C may be useful. Once absorbed, vitamin C is rapidly distributed throughout the body. As with vitamin A, normal cells do not pick up more vitamin C than they need to function.

Since vitamin C is rapidly degraded in the body, the maintenance of effective blood levels may require taking vitamin C at least two times a day.

Vitamin E

Vitamin E can be taken as alpha-tocopherol, in combination with alpha-tocopheryl succinate. Most of alpha-tocopheryl succinate is converted to alpha-tocopherol in the lumen of the intestine prior to being absorbed; however, a portion of alpha-tocopheryl succinate is absorbed without hydrolysis and appears in the blood as one tenth of alpha-tocopherol. About 20 percent of ingested alpha-tocopherol is absorbed from the small intestine and is rapidly distributed throughout the body. As with vitamins A and C, normal cells do not pick up greater amounts of alpha-tocopherol or alpha-tocopheryl succinate than they need.

Since the maximum levels of alpha-tocopherol in the blood appear four to six hours after it is ingested and drop to a basal level in about twelve hours, the maintenance of higher blood levels of vitamin E requires taking it twice a day (morning and evening).

Which vitamins should we take, how much, and how often?

At this time, the doses of vitamins for the greatest benefit to human health or for maximum reduction of cancer risk are unknown. Recommended Daily Allowances (RDA) for vitamins and other nutrients are listed in Tables 4–7.

At present there are two opinions regarding the importance of these current RDA values. One group of scientists believes that RDA values are adequate for maintaining good human health and that larger amounts of vitamins may be harmful. Another group of scientists believes that the current RDA values for vitamins are adequate to prevent deficiency, but that larger amounts may be needed to maintain good health and especially to prevent cancer. Experimental results from animal studies support the view that higher doses are needed for cancer prevention.

Even though we do not have sufficient scientific information regarding doses of vitamins needed to reduce the risk of cancer in human beings, interim guidelines for taking supplemental vitamins have been developed for the following reasons:

1. Adequate animal data are already available.

2. Adequate human data will not become available for many, many years. Many of us cannot wait that long.

3. Without interim guidelines the individual must assess his or her own needs for dietary and supplemental vitamins. Some studies have estimated that 40 percent of all Americans take supplemental vitamins and other nutrients on a regular basis. When one talks with some of these people, one can see that many are consuming nutrients in amounts that may not be helpful and may even be harmful.

TABLE 4: RECOMMENDED DAILY ALLOWANCES (RDA) FOR VITAMINS

VITAMINS		RDA
Vitamin A	Men	3,300 I.U.
	Women	2,600 I.U.
	Pregnant women	2,600 I.U.
Vitamin C	Men	60 mg
	Women	60 mg
	Pregnant women	70 mg
	Smokers	100 mg
Vitamin E	Men	10 I.U.
	Women	8 I.U.
	Pregnant women	10 I.U.
Vitamin D	Men	200 I.U.
	Women	200 I.U.
	Pregnant women	400 I.U.
Vitamin K	Men and women	80 µg
Thiamine	Men	1.22 mg
	Women	1.03 mg
	Pregnant women	1.53 mg
Pantothenic Acid	Men and women	4–7 mg (estimated)
Biotin	Men and women	30–100 µg
Riboflavin	Men and women	1.2 mg
	Pregnant women	1.5 mg
Niacin	Men and women	13 mg
	Pregnant women	13 mg
Vitamin B_6	Men	2.0 mg
	Women	1.6 mg
	Pregnant women	2.2 mg
Folate	Men	200 µg
	Women	180 µg
	Pregnant women	400 µg
Vitamin B_{12}	Men and women	2 µg
	Pregnant women	2.2 µg

mg = milligram   µg = microgram   I.U. = International Unit

TABLE 5: RECOMMENDED DAILY ALLOWANCES (RDA) FOR TRACE METALS

TRACE METALS		RDA
Iron	Men and postmeno- pausal women	10 mg
	Women	15 mg
	Pregnant women	30 mg
Zinc	Men	15 mg
	Women	12 mg
	Pregnant women	15 mg
Iodine	Men	150 µg
	Women	150 µg
	Pregnant women	175 µg
Copper	Men and women	1.5 mg
Manganese	Men and women	2.0–5 mg
Fluoride	Men and women	1.5–4 mg
Chromium	Men and women	50–200 µg
Molybdenum	Men and women	75–250 µg
Selenium	Men	70 µg
	Women	55 µg

TABLE 6: RECOMMENDED DAILY ALLOWANCES (RDA) FOR MINERALS

MINERALS		RDA
Calcium	Men and women	800 mg
	Pregnant women	1,200 mg
Phosphorus	Men and women	800 mg
	Pregnant women	1,200 mg
Magnesium	Men	350 mg
	Women	280 mg
	Pregnant women	300 mg

Table 7: Recommended Daily Allowances (RDA) for Nutrients

NUTRIENTS	RDA
Carbohydrate	No specific requirements, 287 grams for men, 117 grams for women (estimated intake)
Fiber	No specific requirements, 12 grams
Proteins	0.75 gram per kilogram of body weight; or 56.3 grams for a 75 kilogram (165 pounds) person (estimated intake)
Fats	No specific requirements, about 36.4 percent of total calories (estimated intake)
Calories	2,300–2,900 for men, 1,900–2,200 for women

INTERIM GUIDELINES FOR SUPPLEMENTAL VITAMINS

The following doses and dose schedules of beta-carotene and vitamins A, C, and E are based on animal and human studies and are unlikely to produce any major side effects in the average normal human. They may also reduce the risk of cancer.

Beta-carotene

A daily dose of 15 mg taken orally. This is equivalent to 25,000 I.U. of vitamin A if all beta-carotenes become converted to retinol at the same time; however, this does not happen.

Vitamin A

A total of 5,000 I.U. per day, taken orally, divided into two doses, once in the morning and once in the evening (each dose containing 2,500 I.U. of retinyl acetate.

The average dietary consumption of vitamin A by Americans

is about 2,500 I.U. per day. An additional consumption of 5,000 I.U. will probably not produce any side effects.

The reason for taking vitamin A twice a day is that blood levels of vitamin A reach a maximum level in three to six hours and drop to an original level ten to twelve hours after inges-tion. Thus, in order to maintain sustained high levels of vitamin A in the blood an oral intake of vitamin A twice a day is needed.

Both beta-carotene and retinyl acetate have been included in the supplemental vitamin recommendations because beta-caro-tene, in addition to being a precursor of retinol, appears to have some other actions of its own.

Vitamin C

A total of 1 gram per day, taken orally, divided into at least two doses (each dose containing 500 milligrams of vitamin C).

The average dietary consumption of vitamin C by Americans is about 20–40 milligrams per day. A total daily intake of 1 gram plus 20–40 milligrams of dietary vitamin C will probably not produce any side effects.

The reason for taking vitamin C at least two times a day is that blood levels of vitamin C rise rapidly after its ingestion and drop to an original level four to six hours later. Thus, in order to maintain a sustained high level of vitamin C in the blood, an intake of vitamin C at least twice a day is needed.

Vitamin E

A total of 200–400 I.U. per day, taken orally, divided into two doses, one in the morning and one in the evening (each dose containing 50–100 I.U. of alpha-tocopheryl succinate and 50–100 I.U. of alpha-tocopherol).

The average dietary consumption of vitamin E by Americans is about 10–20 I.U. per day. There is no evidence that an additional daily intake of 200–400 I.U. of vitamin E will produce any side effects.

The reason for taking vitamin E twice a day is that blood levels of vitamin E reach a maximum level about four to six hours after ingestion and drop to an original level ten to twelve hours after ingestion. Thus, in order to maintain sustained high levels of vitamin E in the blood, an oral intake of vitamin E twice a day is needed.

Both alpha-tocopherol and alpha-tocopheryl succinate have been included because alpha-tocopheryl succinate cannot act as an antioxidant until it is converted to the alpha-tocopherol form. Thus, the presence of alpha-tocopherol in the intestinal tract is necessary in order to block carcinogenic events such as the formation of nitrosamines in the stomach, and mutagenic substances in the intestine. In addition, alpha-tocopheryl succinate has been found to be the most effective form of vitamin E, at least in experimental systems. Recent studies suggest that some cells, especially in the brain, preferentially pick up natural forms of vitamin E. However, as yet this has not been demonstrated in humans.

Do we need supplementary vitamins if we have a balanced diet?

For nutrition, no; for cancer prevention, probably yes.

One would have difficulty eating fresh fruits and vegetables daily in the amounts and at frequencies that would maintain sustained high levels of beta-carotene and vitamins A, C, and E in the blood; therefore, consumption of supplemental vitamins in addition to eating a balanced diet is essential.

An advantage of taking supplemental vitamins is that one can take them at the most appropriate time to prevent the formation of cancer-causing agents and reduce their carcinogenic effects, especially just before eating food containing nitrites or other cancer-causing substances.

Some scientists believe that a balanced diet is sufficient to maintain good health and prevent disease. However, recent studies suggest that all naturally occurring foods have toxic substances as well as protective substances inherent in their constitution; therefore, a balanced diet alone may not be sufficient for disease prevention. While a balanced diet is better than junk food and will prevent vitamin deficiency, the main problem with the concept of a balanced diet is that it is very general, and the interpretation of this concept may vary markedly from one individual to another. Some persons may believe that a daily intake of one apple, one carrot, one orange, some fresh vegetables, meat and carbohydrates constitutes a balanced diet; whereas others may believe that a balanced diet should contain more or less of those items. Thus, the concept that a balanced diet is adequate for maximum protection against cancer may not be correct.

Even if a balanced diet is defined more precisely, the same balanced diet cannot be applied to all the regions of the world because dietary and environmental levels of precursors* of cancer-causing substances, tumor promoters, and tumor initiators vary markedly from one region to another. Thus, supplemental vitamins may be necessary to reduce the risk of cancer.

With respect to cancer prevention, ingesting certain vitamins at the right time is important; otherwise their possible effectiveness against cancer may be minimized. For example, vitamins C and E, if taken immediately before eating food containing nitrites, may reduce the formation of nitrosamines in the stomach. Taking these vitamins a few hours after such a meal may not effectively interfere with this stage of carcinogenesis. Furthermore, studies have demonstrated that levels of fecal mutagens (a possible source of cancer) in persons who regularly eat meat are much higher than in those who are vegetarians. Ingestion of vitamin C and vitamin E has been shown to reduce the levels of mutagens in the feces. Therefore,

---

* Some chemicals do not cause cancer until they are converted to a cancer-causing form. These chemicals are called precursors.

these vitamins should be taken before or right after eating meat. Taking these vitamins several hours after such a meal may not be very effective.

In addition, when one travels or vacations away from home, the quantities of fresh fruits and vegetables needed to provide sufficient vitamins may not be available. Thus, supplemental vitamins are also needed under these conditions.

The absolute amounts of vitamins may not be important in cancer prevention. Instead, the relative levels of cancer-causing substances present in the diet and the environment and anticancer substances such as vitamins and selenium in the body are crucial in determining the potential for cancer. Consequently, increased consumption of cancer-causing substances via diet and environment would require a proportional increase in available anticancer substances.

All types of diets including those that are defined as balanced diets contain both toxic and protective substances. Some of the toxic agents such as pesticides are synthetic, whereas others are naturally occurring. Therefore, the risk of chronic illness, including cancer, may depend upon the relative consumption of protective and toxic substances. If the daily intake levels of protective substances are higher than toxic agents, the incidence of chronic illness would be reduced. Since we know very little about the relative levels of toxic and protective substances in any diet, we cannot know whether we are consuming daily higher levels of protective substances in comparison to toxic ones. To assure a higher intake of protective agents, a daily supplement of vitamins is needed.

RISKS OF TAKING VITAMINS

Beta-carotene

There is no known toxicity of beta-carotene up to 30 milligrams per day. The bronzing of skin may appear after oral ingestion of beta-carotene at 100 milligrams per day or more over a long period of time. These changes are reversible after discontinuation.

Vitamin A

Liver toxicity and skin reactions have been noted after oral ingestion of 50,000 I.U. per day of vitamin A over a long period of time. Some of these changes are reversible after the practice is discontinued. Dosages of up to 10,000 I.U. of vitamin A taken orally and divided into two doses per day, are unlikely to produce any major toxic effects in an average normal adult. Pregnant women should avoid taking more than 5,000 I.U. of vitamin A because higher doses may produce adverse effects on the fetus.

Vitamin C

In most healthy persons, doses of vitamin C up to 10 grams per day taken orally do not produce any detectable toxic effects. However, in certain diseases involving iron metabolism (hemochromatosis), copper metabolism (Wilson's disease), and excessive exposure to manganese (Parkinsonian-like syndrome), an excessive consumption of vitamin C may be harmful, because vitamin C in combination with iron, copper, or manganese, in the presence of oxygen, generates free radicals (harmful chemical species). According to many studies, dosages up to 2 grams of vitamin C, taken orally and divided into at least two doses per day, are unlikely to cause any serious side effects in an average normal adult.

Vitamin E

In a large human trial involving nine thousand adults, a daily oral intake of 3,000 I.U. per day of alpha-tocopherol acetate for eleven years did not produce any detectable major side effects; however, isolated cases of fatigue, skin reactions, and upset stomach have been reported after ingestion of high doses (above

1,000 I.U. daily) of vitamin E for a prolonged period of time. According to many studies, dosages up to 400 I.U. of vitamin E taken orally, divided into two doses per day, are unlikely to produce any major toxic effects in an average normal adult.

DIETARY FIBER AND REDUCED CANCER RISK

Some human and animal studies suggest that a diet containing high levels of fiber may reduce the risk of certain cancers, especially large bowel (colon and rectal) cancer. The incidence of these cancers is virtually absent among people of northwest India (Punjabi) who eat a diet rich in roughage, cellulose, vegetables, fiber, and yogurt, in comparison with southern Indians who do not eat such foods. Also, as noted previously, the incidence of cancer in general is much lower among Seventh Day Adventists, who are vegetarians. A diet high in fiber results in regular bowel movements, which reduce the body's contact time with cancer-causing substances normally formed in the intestinal tract. This may reduce the absorption of carcinogens and thereby reduce the risk of cancer.

In a randomized, double-blind, placebo-controlled trial, patients with familial adenomatous polyposis (precancerous lesions of colon cancer) who consumed an average of 22 grams total of fiber and vitamin C (4 grams per day) and alpha-tocopherol (400 milligrams per day) were found to show a decrease in the number of polyps in comparison to those who received either vitamins plus low fiber (2.2 grams per day) or those who received low fiber plus placebo. Reports show that only 10 percent of the United States population consumes more than 20 grams of dietary fiber daily.

SELENIUM

How does selenium prevent cancer?
Small amounts of selenium are absolutely essential for good health, and among minerals only selenium has been shown to have a role in cancer prevention. The very limited data for human beings tend to confirm the anticancer effects of selenium.

Like vitamin E, selenium in combination with glutathione peroxidase acts as an antioxidant and strengthens the body's immune defense system. Thus, many of the effects that are produced by vitamin E deficiency can be reversed or prevented by selenium. Some laboratory results have suggested that a combination of vitamin E and selenium is more effective in preventing cancer than either of them alone.

Metals that block the action of selenium
Certain metals such as lead, cadmium, arsenic, mercury, and silver block the action of selenium.

A common belief is that high doses of zinc are very good for maintaining health, but this may not be true with respect to cancer prevention. Recent laboratory experiments have shown that high doses of zinc block the action of selenium. Therefore, one has to be careful about taking excessive amounts of zinc (more than 20 milligrams total per day from diet and supplements) while taking selenium.

Nutrients that increase selenium requirements
Protein-rich and unsaturated fat-rich diets have been shown to increase the selenium requirements of the body.

These studies suggest that to get the greatest cancer preventing benefits of selenium, a diet low in those metals that block the action of selenium, and one that provides adequate but not excessive amounts of zinc, protein and unsaturated fats should be considered.

How to select supplementary selenium
Commercial preparations of selenium include inorganic selenium (sodium selenite) and various organic compounds of selenium. Some have reported that sodium selenite is not absorbed adequately, whereas organic selenium, including yeast-selenium, is absorbed very well. For this reason, organic selenium is considered best for human consumption.

Table 8: Summary of the Actions of Vitamins and Selenium in Cancer Prevention

NUTRIENTS	PREVENTIVE ACTION
Vitamin C and vitamin E (alpha-tocopherol)	Block the formation of cancer-causing agents.
	Block the conversion of some cancer-causing agents to active forms.
Beta-carotene, vitamin A (retinol and retinoic acid), vitamin C, vitamin E (alpha-tocopherol, alpha-tocopheryl succinate), and selenium	Block the action of tumor-causing agents (initiators and promoters).
Beta-carotene, vitamins A, C, and E	Reverse newly formed cancer cells back to normal cells.
Beta-carotene, vitamins A, C, E, and selenium	Kill newly formed cancer cells in the body by stimulating the body's immune defense system.

How much selenium should one take and how often?
The optimal doses of selenium for health benefits are unknown. The current average dietary intake of selenium is 125–150

micrograms per day. The RDA value of selenium for adults is 55–70 micrograms per day. Selenium dosages of about 250–300 micrograms per day (diet and supplements) have been reported helpful in preventing cancer. If an average person already consumes 125–150 micrograms of selenium per day, an additional supplement of 100 micrograms per day is unlikely to produce any major side effects.

Risks of taking selenium
Animal studies suggest that 2–3 micrograms per gram of diet (twenty to thirty times the human RDA) per day may produce toxic side effects. The window of safety for selenium is very narrow. The total daily intake (diet and supplement) of 500 micrograms or more of selenium may be toxic to humans.

NUTRIENTS THAT MAY INCREASE THE RISK OF CANCER

Excess total fat
Both human studies and animal experiments suggest that increasing the intake of total fat increases the risk of certain cancers, particularly breast, colon, prostate, and possibly other cancers. Conversely, lowering fat intake reduces the risk of these cancers. Data from animal studies suggest that when total fat intake is low, polyunsaturated fats are more likely than saturated fats to cause cancer. However, the relevance of this observation for human beings is not clear at this time. In addition, specific components of fat responsible for enhanced carcinogenesis have not been identified, although some studies have indicated that excess cholesterol consumption may increase the risk of cancer. Extensive human studies are needed to define the role of excess cholesterol in carcinogenesis.

The exact reasons for the effects of a high-fat diet on cancer risk are unknown. However, some recent laboratory experiments have reported that the production of prostaglandin E2 (PGE2), a chemical that is normally produced by the body, is markedly increased in animals that are fed a high fat diet. High levels of PGE2 have been shown to impair the body's immune defense system. Therefore, the increased risk of cancer brought about by a high-fat diet may be due to the suppression of the body's defense system against cancer. High fat can also act as a tumor promoter.

Also high doses of vitamin E have been reported to reduce the production of PGE2, and consequently high doses of vitamin E may block the harmful effects of excessive fat consumption. This does not mean that one should continue eating a high-fat diet and take large amounts of vitamin E. Such practices may be very harmful because a high-fat diet may increase the risk of heart attack.

The presence of excessive amounts of bile acids and fatty acids may promote colon cancer because they increase the proliferation of cells in the colon. Increased cell proliferation is considered a risk factor for colon cancer. Dietary calcium inhibits the above action of bile acids and fatty acids by precipitating them and thus rendering them unavailable for absorption.

Excess protein

Based on limited laboratory and human studies, an excessive intake of protein may be associated with an increased risk of cancer of the breast, endometrium, prostate, colon, rectum, pancreas, and kidney. A lower protein intake seems to reduce the risk of cancer. Although animal studies suggest a specific role for protein in carcinogenesis, human studies are not convincing. Since the Western diet contains significant amounts of meat, which is a rich source of both protein and fat, determining an independent role for protein in human carcinogenesis is difficult at this time. However, the fact that animal experiments show that high protein intake increases the incidence of chemically induced tumors indicates that proteins may have a similar role in human cancer. Additional studies are needed to substantiate this particular point.

Excess total calories and excess carbohydrates

There are some limited studies that suggest that increased total caloric intake may increase the risk of cancer, but the data on both animals and human beings are sparse and indirect. Further studies are needed to answer this question.

There are no scientific data to suggest that an excessive intake of carbohydrates is directly related to the risk of cancer in animals or in human beings. However, excessive consumption of carbohydrates may increase total caloric intake. Additional studies are needed to define the role of carbohydrates in human carcinogenesis.

HOW TO DESIGN YOUR NUTRITION AND LIFESTYLE PROGRAM TO REDUCE THE RISK OF CANCER

Several scientific agencies such as the National Academy of Science, American Cancer Society, and the American Institute for Cancer Research have published diet guidelines for reducing cancer risk. These contain very useful information but no recommendations as yet for supplementary vitamins. The Cancer Research Institute, New York, has also prepared diet guidelines that contain recommendations for supplementary vitamins and other nutrients. Even though there are no solid human data that suggest that supplemental beta-carotene; vitamins A, C, and E, and selenium are essential for reducing the risk of cancer, there are sufficient animal and limited human studies that indicate that interim guidelines for supplementary vitamins and minerals should also be developed.

Interim guidelines for diet

1. Increase consumption of fresh fruits and vegetables.
2. Increase consumption of fiber by consuming up to 22 grams per day.
3. Reduce fat consumption to 20 percent of total calories (1 gram of fat equals nine calories).
4. Avoid excessive consumption of protein, carbohydrates, and calories.
5. Reduce consumption of food with high nitrate or nitrite content. Whenever eating such foods, take 250 milligrams of vitamin C or drink fresh orange juice before eating.
6. Avoid eating excessive amounts of charcoal-broiled or smoked meat or fish.
7. Reduce consumption of pickled fruits and vegetables.

Table 9 describes some vitamin-rich fruits and vegetables that can be eaten for breakfast, lunch, and dinner.

TABLE 9: INTERIM DIETARY GUIDELINES

BREAKFAST

- Fiber-rich cereals with low-fat or skim milk, or whole wheat toast.
- Fruits rich in beta-carotene such as apricots, mangoes, peaches, or cantaloupes.
- Fruits rich in vitamin C such as oranges, pineapples, strawberries, or raspberries.

LUNCH

- One piece skinless chicken, other meats, or fish.
- Rolls, toast, or rice.
- Fruits, as in breakfast.
- Two vegetables from asparagus, spinach, broccoli, cabbage, corn, cauliflower, peas, beans, brussels sprouts, or potatoes
- Salad containing spinach, parsley, cucumbers, tomatoes, with a small amount of vitamin E-rich oils (wheat germ, sunflower, or olive).

DINNER

- Same categories as lunch.
- In addition, two fruits of your choice, one glass of low-fat or skim milk, and low-calorie dessert.

INTERIM GUIDELINES FOR SUPPLEMENTARY NUTRITION

Beta-carotene

15 milligrams per day, taken orally, once a day.

Vitamin A

5,000 I.U. per day, taken orally, divided into two doses—once in the morning and once in the evening (each dose containing 2,500 I.U. of retinyl acetate).

Vitamin C

1 gram per day, divided into at least two doses, each containing 500 milligrams of vitamin C in powder or tablet form, taken orally.

Vitamin E

200–400 I.U. per day, divided into two doses, each dose containing 50–100 I.U. of alpha-tocopherol and 50–100 I.U. of alpha-tocopheryl succinate, taken orally, twice a day.

Selenium

100 micrograms of organic selenium per day, divided into two doses.

Other Vitamins

B vitamins are important for our health. Therefore these vitamins may be taken in amounts higher than RDA (2–5 times depending upon the vitamins).

INTERIM LIFESTYLE GUIDELINES

1. Avoid drinking excessive amounts of alcohol, caffeinated or decaffeinated coffee, and tea.

2. DO NOT SMOKE. Avoid exposure to passive smoke. Do not chew tobacco products.

3. Exercise daily for twenty to thirty minutes. If you do aerobic exercise for thirty minutes or more, take vitamin supplements beforehand.

4. Adopt a lifestyle of reduced stress.

5. Avoid excessive sun exposure.

At this time, children should not be given supplemental vitamins or selenium in the amounts recommended for an average normal adult. However, a daily intake of one multiple vitamin containing RDA amounts is recommended for children. The diet and lifestyle guidelines may be equally useful for children except that the fat intake may be limited to about 30 percent of total calories. Fiber should be consumed through eating fruits, vegetables, and fiber-rich cereals.

ADDITIONAL BENEFITS OF FOLLOWING A CANCER PREVENTION PROGRAM

Adapting one's diet, supplementary nutrition, and lifestyle for cancer prevention is not limited *only* to cancer protection. Such a program may also be very useful for maintaining sound health, possibly because vitamins protect the body against injurious effects of agents that do not cause cancer. For example, accidental consumption of excess mercury compounds has produced severe neurological diseases in human beings. Lower doses of mercury compounds may cause behavioral disturbances. Some laboratory experiments suggest that vitamin E reduces the risk of developing neurological diseases when supplemental vitamins are given to animals during exposure to mercury compounds.

Free radicals are produced normally in the body. Some of these free radicals are needed to maintain certain vital cell functions. However, if free radicals are produced in excess, either because of genetic defects or through consumption of agents that generate large quantities of free radicals in the body, some vital organs may be permanently damaged. The presence of beta-carotene; vitamins A, C, and E; and selenium in the body in sufficient amounts may protect these organs against the injurious effects of free radicals.

Some scientists have proposed that an imbalance between the amounts of free radicals produced and available amounts of beta-carotene; vitamins A, C, and E; and selenium may be responsible for normal aging processes (i.e., more free radicals and fewer vitamins and selenium may increase the rate of aging). If this is the case, the presence of sufficient amounts of these nutrients may reduce the damage and thereby reduce the rate of some degenerative changes associated with aging, especially in the brain. The proposed changes in diet, lifestyle, and supplementary nutrition may also reduce the risk of heart disease and eye defects (cataracts). A human study published in 1993 has shown that the supplementation with vitamin E reduces the risk of heart diseases.

COMMON WAYS IN WHICH VITAMINS AND OTHER NUTRIENTS ARE MISUSED

1. In recent years many nutrition books have been published, and some contain erroneous information regarding doses and dose-schedules for supplementary nutrients. Thus, careful selection of a book by which to prepare your diet guidelines

is important. Make sure that the credentials of the authors include research, patient care, and teaching expertise in the area of vitamins and nutrition.

2. Base your estimate of vitamins and nutrients for daily consumption on your needs and check with a physician who is knowledgeable in this area to see if your estimates are reasonable.

3. Do not buy any vitamins or nutrients that are not fully described on the label.

4. Do not take excessive amounts of nutrients that will make you sick. Some nutrition books have suggested that one should increase the doses in the beginning until some kind of sickness is manifested, then decrease the doses until a comfortable level is reached. This is very dangerous, as some nutrients in large amounts can cause irreversible damage.

5. If you have further questions, consult experts who are actively involved in research, teaching, or patient care (see pages 87–98).

The above considerations will make your efforts to improve your health and to reduce the risk of cancer more effective and less expensive.

3

Treating Cancer

WHAT IS THE CURRENT STATUS OF CANCER THERAPY?

Before discussing the role of vitamins in the treatment of cancer, one should understand the nature of cancer cells and the current status, usefulness, and limitations of different kinds of therapy.

Are all cells of a cancer similar?

If all cells of a cancer were similar, treating cancer would be easy, because one therapeutic agent would be sufficient to kill all of the cells. Unfortunately, cancer cells are very complex in the sense that there are many different kinds of cells within the same cancer. Therefore, a variety of drugs that have different modes of action are commonly used in treating cancer. This approach kills more cancer cells than would be killed by a single agent.

Many have repeatedly observed that cancer cells may become very unresponsive to *all* therapeutic agents after a period of good initial response. This is because almost all of the agents used to treat cancer also *cause* cancer themselves. During treatment these agents produce many biochemical changes among those cancer cells that are not killed and make them "super cancer cells." Such "super cancer cells" cannot be killed, even by a more poisonous chemical.

Thus, tumors contains cells many of which are different from each other. Some differences are inherent (i.e., they are present before treatment), whereas other differences are acquired (i.e., they are produced by treatment agents). From these observations we can clearly see that the complexity of tumor cells increases during the treatment phase and that no single agent may ever be sufficient to cure tumors.

BENEFITS AND LIMITATIONS OF VARIOUS TREATMENTS

Current cancer therapies include surgery, chemotherapy, radiation therapy, heat therapy, and treatment with monoclonal antibodies (a kind of protein that is supposed to kill specific cancer cells without killing normal cells). Frequently surgery is used in combination with chemotherapy and radiation, or in combination with chemotherapy, radiation, and heat. Monoclonal antibodies are being used as an experimental drug in the treatment of certain cancers. The usefulness and limitations of each of these agents are discussed below.

Surgery
Surgery is one of the most commonly used procedures in the

treatment of solid cancers that are accessible to such treatment. However, many cancer sites are not accessible and even when they are, minute, invisible tumors are likely to be left in the body. Nevertheless, surgery is considered one of the best available approaches to cancer therapy because it does not significantly increase the risk of later developing new cancer or noncancer diseases.

Chemotherapy

Many toxic chemicals are used extensively in treating cancer, frequently in combination with surgery and radiation. Almost all of them kill both cancer cells and normal cells, cause severe illness, destroy the body's immune defense system, and increase the risk of new cancer among patients who survive more than five years.

Reports show that the incidence of leukemia (blood cancer) and solid tumors among the survivors of chemotherapy and radiation therapy is about 10 percent. However, the observation periods upon which this figure is based are usually no more than ten years after completion of treatment. According to present knowledge, the risk of additional leukemia may not increase any further, but the risk of developing new solid cancers and noncancerous diseases persists up to thirty years or more after treatment. In spite of these limitations, chemotherapy must be used until better treatment methods are established.

Radiation Therapy

Radiation is commonly used in treating human cancer. It is frequently used in combination with surgery or chemotherapy, or both. Like chemotherapy, radiation produces toxic effects. It kills both normal and cancer cells, causes severe illness, destroys the body's immune defense system, and increases the risk of new cancer among those who survive. Generally the time interval between radiation exposure and detection of new tumors is about ten years for leukemia and up to thirty years or more for solid tumors. The risk of developing noncancerous diseases also persists long after completion of treatment (usually more than fifteen years). In spite of these limitations, radiation must be used until better treatment methods are established.

Heat Therapy

Generally temperatures of 42°–43° C (107.6°–109.4° F) are used in heat therapy, primarily for the purpose of controlling local tumors. However, raising the whole-body temperature from 37° C (98.6° F) to 42° C or 43° C would be lethal. Heat is frequently used in combination with radiation therapy. This approach has provided occasional relief for some patients when other treatment methods were ineffective, but in general, results have been disappointing. Some recent laboratory experiments suggest that the use of high temperatures (42°–43° C) in combination with radiation may actually increase the incidence of radiation-induced cancer. Because of these limitations, the use of high temperatures (over 41° C or 105.8° F) cannot be considered in designing long-term treatment strategies for human cancer. However, the use of heat therapy at a lower temperature (40° C or 104° F), in combination with nontoxic chemicals that increase the effect of heat, may be of some value in treating human cancer, because the whole-body temperature can be raised from 37° to 40° C without toxic effects.

Monoclonal Antibody Therapy

Monoclonal antibodies, a kind of immune protein are produced by biotechnology companies. We assume that such monoclonal antibodies will kill primarily cancer cells that bind to these antibodies. Unfortunately, these antibodies are not specific for cancer cells; they also bind with many normal cells. Thus, the usefulness of antibodies in treating cancer is limited. Nevertheless, if even a small percentage of cancer cells is killed by such a selective means, continued research and development of this method are justified.

Current treatment methods have produced increasing numbers of long-term survivors of early stage diseases, such as Hodgkin's disease, childhood leukemia, Wilms' tumor (kidney), cervical cancer, prostate cancer, neuroblastoma, retinoblastoma (eye tumor), and melanoma (skin cancer). The risk of future consequence exists in these "cured" patients. In most other cancers, current treatment agents have been less effective.

Delayed Consequences of Cancer Therapies

Based on a five-year survival rate, significant progress has been made in the treatment of some cancers. But if one considers recent indications of an increased risk of developing new cancer and noncancer diseases, one becomes concerned about the consequences and adequacy of current methods of treatment. Noncancerous diseases that may afflict survivors include the following:

Aplastic anemia—if the bone marrow was involved during therapy.

Paralysis—if the spinal cord was involved during therapy.

Cataract—if one or both eyes were involved during therapy.

Reproductive failures—if the gonads were involved during therapy.

Necrosis—in nondividing organs such as the brain, liver, and muscle cells, if they were involved during therapy.

Retardation of growth—if the patient was a child.

Because of these potential risks, newer approaches to cancer treatments that utilize nontoxic agents *must* be developed. However, it should be emphasized that current methods of treatment *must be continued,* despite potential risks, until better therapies are developed.

BETTER METHODS OF CANCER TREATMENT

The best ways to treat cancer would be to transform all cancer cells to normal cells, or to kill all cancers cells without killing normal cells, or both. In order to achieve the first goal, we need to understand the basic steps involved in maintaining the regular features of normal cells and the basic events by which normal cells *become* cancer cells. In order to achieve the second goal, we need to identify nontoxic substances that kill cancer cells without killing normal cells. If one considers the evolution of cancer cells in the body, nontoxic agents that change cancer cells to normal cells and that kill only tumor cells, in theory, may be found. For example, the transformation from normal cells to cancer cells probably occurs more frequently than we realize; however, these newly formed cancer cells do not always develop into detectable cancer, possibly because the body has an elaborate defense system, which includes the immune system. When cancer cells escape the body's defense system, they continue to grow and become detectable. If we can identify those substances that stimulate the body's defense system, we can possibly kill tumor cells selectively without killing normal cells.

WHY VITAMINS?

Numerous laboratory experiments indicate that there are several nontoxic and naturally occurring substances that change some cancer cells back to normal cells and that kill cancer cells *without* killing normal cells. These include beta-carotene and vitamins A, C, and E. The following sections describe the importance of vitamins in treating cancer, alone and in combination with currently used tumor therapeutic agents.

Laboratory studies have led to clinical trials of vitamins, primarily beta-carotene and vitamins A, C, and E, in treating certain human cancers. Preliminary results show that high doses of each of these vitamins reduce the growth of tumors. At this time we do not know fully whether a combination of beta-carotene and vitamins A, C, and E is more effective in reducing tumor growth than the vitamins individually. Laboratory experiments suggest that vitamins may markedly improve cancer treatment in the following ways:

1. Reducing tumor growth without affecting normal cells.
2. Transforming some cancer cells to normal cells.
3. Enhancing the cell-killing effects of currently used chemotherapeutic agents, radiation, and heat.
4. Reducing some of the toxic side effects radiation and certain chemotherapeutic agents have on normal cells.
5. Stimulating the body's immune defense system.

The extent and type of effect that vitamins have depend upon the type, form, dosage, and method of administration, as well as the type and stage of tumor. The importance of individual vitamins in treating cancer is discussed below.

Beta-carotene and Vitamin A

Both beta-carotene and vitamin A (13-cis retinoic acid, an analog of retinoic acid) inhibit the growth of some cancer cells *in vitro*. They also convert some cancer cells to normal cells *in vitro*. Beta-carotene at a dose of 180 milligrams per week produced complete remission of cancer in 15 percent of patients with oral leukoplakia. The combination of beta-carotene and vitamin A (100,000 I.U. per week) caused complete remission in 27 percent of those patients in comparison to a placebo group in which complete remission was observed in only 3 percent. A higher dose of vitamin A alone (13-cis-retinoic acid at 200,000 I.U. per week) produced complete remission in 27 percent of patients with oral leukoplakia.

The recurrence of melanoma after surgical removal of the primary tumor is high (30–75 percent), depending upon the stage of the cancer. Reports show that the combination of BCG vaccine with vitamin A (100,000 I.U. per day) for eighteen months slightly increases the period of disease-free time in melanoma (stages 1 and 2) more than BCG vaccine alone. The side effects of this treatment included dry skin and mild depression.

A pronounced beneficial effect of 13-cis-retinoic acid on cutaneous T-cell lymphoma (mycosis fungoides) was observed. Eight of twelve patients responded well, with four showing a nearly complete cure from the disease. Beneficial effects of vitamin A were also observed on patients with epithelial tumors. Some epithelial tumor cells are resistant to vitamin A; the reasons for their resistance are unknown. Vitamin A was ineffective in treating nonepithelial cancer. Further studies are needed to evaluate the role of beta-carotene and vitamin A in the treatment of human cancers. It is certain that both beta-carotene and vitamin A by themselves will not be sufficient in the treatment of advanced cancer.

Vitamin C

Although vitamin C has been shown to reduce the growth of animal tumors, its role in treating human cancer has become controversial. Cameron and Pauling have reported that the administration of high doses of sodium ascorbate (5–10 grams per day) increases the survival of patients with advanced cancer. These patients were either treated minimally with conventional therapies or not treated at all. Other scientists have reported that high doses of vitamin C were ineffective in improving the survival of patients with terminal cancer. These patients were treated extensively with radiation and chemotherapy before being given vitamin C. Thus, the difference in results may be due to the fact that in the patients of Cameron and Pauling the tumor contained cells that were sensitive to vitamin C; whereas in the other patients the tumors contained cells that became more complex because of treatment with chemicals and radiation, and thus were resistant to vitamin C. Therefore, the treatment of cancer with vitamin C alone may possibly be of some value when it is given before radiation or chemotherapy.

A recent study in Japan has reported that local infusion of sodium ascorbate with copper and glycyl-glycyl-histidine, a peptide (protein), caused complete regression of osteosarcoma (bone cancer) in a patient. This observation is very exciting and calls for further research. We should point out, however, that vitamin C alone may never be sufficient in the treatment of human cancer.

Vitamin E

Laboratory experiments have shown that alpha-tocopheryl succinate causes some cancer cells to revert to normal and that it inhibits the growth of several other cancer cells. Other forms of vitamin E such as alpha-tocopherol, alpha-tocopheryl acetate, and alpha-tocopheryl nicotinate at similar doses were ineffective. However, cancer cells that are resistant to alpha-tocopheryl succinate do exist, and the reasons for their resistance are unknown. The extent and type of effect depend upon the form of cancer and the form of vitamin E.

In a recent clinical trial, high doses of alpha-tocopherol were used to treat human neuroblastoma that had become unresponsive to all standard therapeutic agents. Reports show that more than 50 percent of these patients showed partial regression of their cancer.

We should point out that the alpha-tocopherol that is being

used may not be the most potent form of vitamin E. In view of the fact that those who received vitamin E therapy were all patients who were terminally ill in spite of receiving all available therapy, the preliminary results noted above should be considered encouraging. Further preclinical and clinical studies using alpha-tocopheryl succinate must be performed.

Some other clinical studies suggest that administering high doses of vitamin E is also useful in patients with chronic cystic mastitis, the most common benign tumor of the female breast. However, some studies have failed to confirm the above results. Vitamin E also causes regression of oral leukoplakia in humans. While using vitamin E in clinical or experimental studies, researchers must consider the following:

a. type of vitamin E, alpha-tocopheryl succinate being the most active type of vitamin;

b. form of vitamin E, cells preferentially pick up the natural form of vitamin E (d-form); and

c. dose and dose schedule, 800 I.U. divided into two doses.

Because of the presence of different kinds of cells in a cancer and because beta-carotene and vitamins A, C, and E have, in part, different ways of acting, the combination of these four vitamins may be more effective in the treatment of cancer than the individual vitamins alone. However, no human studies have been performed to test this concept. In a recent human study, the combination of vitamins A, C, and E caused reduction in rate of cell proliferation in colon mucosa (lining of the colon).

Vitamin B$_6$

Some animal studies have reported that supplemental vitamin B$_6$, one of the vitamins of vitamin B complex, enhances the growth of human breast cancer transplanted into nude (no thymus gland) mice and that the restriction of vitamin B$_6$ retards it. The relevance of this observation for human cancer is not known at this time. Nevertheless, supplementation with high doses of vitamin B_6 should be avoided during treatment of breast cancer.

Vitamin D

Some recent laboratory experiments have shown that 1-alpha-hydroxyvitamin D_3 reduces the growth of certain cancers (melanoma, a skin cancer; hepatoma, a liver cancer; myeloid leukemia, a kind of blood cancer) *in vitro*. It also converts some cancer cells, such as human leukemic cells, to cells that are more like normal *in vitro*. Further preclinical and clinical studies are needed to evaluate the role of vitamin D in the treatment of cancer.

The mechanisms by which beta-carotene and vitamins A, C, D, and E reduce the growth or induce differentiation (conversion of cancer cells to cells that are more like normal cells) in cancer cells, are not known. Normal cells may have membrane systems that prevent excessive intake of these vitamins in spite of their high levels in the blood. However, this important membrane system in many cancer cells becomes defective, which then allows the entry of excessive amounts of vitamins. These vitamins in larger amounts may partially or fully shut off oxidation reactions, depending upon their levels inside the cancer cells. For many cellular functions, including the generation of energy and oxidation reactions, oxygen is needed in both normal and cancer cells. Whether vitamins kill cancer cells, reduce the growth of cancer cells, or convert cancer cells to normal cells depends in part upon the degree of inhibition of oxidation reactions inside the cells. If the oxidation reactions are mostly inhibited by vitamins, the cell would die. In addition, these vitamins have actions that are not related to their antioxidation effects.

Modification of the effects of tumor therapeutic agents by beta-carotene and vitamins A, C, and E

Results of laboratory experiments indicate that beta-carotene and vitamins A, C, and E modify (increase or decrease) the effects of therapeutic agents (chemicals, radiation, and heat) on cancer cells. The extent of modification depends upon the types of tumor cells, the types of vitamins, and the types of therapeutic agents.

Cancer therapeutic agents can be grouped into the following categories: radiation, surgery, chemotherapeutic agents, naturally occurring anticancer agents, and heat. The enhancement of the effects of radiation, chemotherapeutic agents, and heat on tumor cells by vitamins is discussed below.

Vitamin A enhances the beneficial effects of radiation and chemotherapy

Animal studies suggest that vitamin A and beta-carotene inhibit the growth of breast cancer in animals. The combination of vitamin A and radiation was more effective than the individual agents. Cancers were completely cured in mice given both vitamin A and radiation. Beta-carotene was equally effective. The combination of cyclophosphamide, a commonly used cancer-therapeutic chemical, with vitamin A or beta-carotene produced a greater regression of tumor growth than did the cyclophosphamide treatment alone. Combining beta-carotene and vitamin A with certain tumor-therapeutic agents may improve the management of cancer, but it has not been tested in human cancers.

Vitamins C enhances the beneficial effects of radiation

Studies have shown that vitamin C increases the effects of radiation on animal neuroblastoma cells, but not on animal glioma cancer cells *in vitro*. Vitamin C in combination with radiation enhances the survival of mice with ascitis (cells in fluid of the abdominal cavity) more than that produced by radiation treatment alone. Also, vitamin C protects Chinese hamster ovary cells against radiation damage. Further studies are needed on these topics.

Vitamin E enhances the beneficial effects of chemotherapeutic agents and radiation

Most currently used chemotherapeutic agents destroy the body's defense system and make people terribly sick. These agents are not normally present in the body but are manufactured synthetically. They kill normal cells as well as cancer cells. Reports show that vitamin E, in combination with currently used chemotherapeutic agents, is more effective on tumor cells than the individual agents alone. However, we must point out that the extent of this kind of effect of vitamin E depends upon the type of cancer and the type of chemotherapeutic agent. If this result is found in human beings, the addition of vitamin E to currently used treatments using chemotherapeutic agents may markedly improve their effectiveness in treating human cancer. Reducing the doses of chemotherapeutic agents required for effective treatment may be possible, and thus the risk of severe sickness decreased. Studies are being initiated to evaluate the role of vitamin E in enhancing the effectiveness of currently used chemotherapies.

Laboratory experiments have shown that alpha-tocopheryl acetate and alpha-tocopheryl succinate increase the effects of radiation on neuroblastoma and glioma (brain tumor). Vitamin E has been shown to protect normal tissue against radiation damage. Furthermore, recent studies show that high doses of alpha-tocopheryl succinate enhance the effects of radiation on tumor cells, whereas low doses of alpha-tocopheryl succinate are ineffective in enhancing the effects of radiation.

These observations suggest that whenever vitamin E is combined with radiation, high doses of alpha-tocopheryl succinate should be used; otherwise, the use of vitamin E may be ineffective. We must point out that the above observations have not been tested extensively on either animal or human cancer. Also, laboratory experiments have shown that there are cancer cells that are resistant to the combined effects of alpha-tocopheryl succinate and radiation.

If vitamins C and E enhance the effects of radiation on human cancer, the addition of these vitamins to radiation therapy may markedly improve its effectiveness and may even reduce the long-term risk of developing new cancer and noncancer diseases. Preclinical and clinical studies should be initiated to test this possibility.

Vitamin E enhances the beneficial effects of naturally occurring anticancer agents

The use of toxic drugs in treating human tumors continues to be emphasized, but it cannot be accepted as the ideal kind of therapy.

An alternative approach must be developed. Recent studies suggest that treating human cancer by using high doses of nontoxic, naturally occurring substances may be possible. These agents at higher concentrations turn some cancer cells into normal cells or reduce the growth of tumors without affecting the normal cells, or both. Some of these are beta-carotene and vitamins A, C, and E (all discussed previously).

In addition to vitamins, two naturally occurring substances, adenosine 3', 5' cyclic monophosphate (cAMP) and butyric acid, have been shown to produce an anticancer effect in the laboratory. The chemical substance cAMP is found in all cells of the body. Several laboratory experiments have suggested that a defect in the cAMP system may be associated with the formation of cancer cells. If this is the case, then the correction of this defect should convert cancer cells to normal cells. Indeed, when this problem in the cAMP system is corrected by using another chemical, the cancer cells of some tumors such as neuroblastoma (a childhood cancer that occurs primarily in the abdomen), melanoma (a skin cancer), oat cell carcinoma (a lung cancer), glioma (a brain cancer), and pheochromocytoma (an adrenal cancer) become normal cells. As expected, not all cells are converted to normal cells by correcting the above defect.

Therefore, an additional study must be performed to find out how the remaining cancer cells can be changed to normal cells. The fact that cancer cells can be converted to normal cells by utilizing cAMP-stimulating agents is very exciting, but the usefulness of this concept in treating human cancer has been tested in only one type of cancer (neuroblastoma). The addition of cAMP-stimulating agents to the treatment protocols for advanced neuroblastoma has shown some encouraging results.

Butyric acid, a small-size fatty acid, occurs in the human body. In cancer experiments, butyric acid is used as sodium butyrate (nonacidic form). Numerous laboratory experiments have shown that sodium butyrate at high doses also converts some cancer cells (erythroid leukemia, a cancer of blood cells) to normal cells. In addition, it kills some other cancer cells without killing normal cells (for example, neuroblastoma, sarcoma, glioma, and melanoma cells). As expected, not all cancer cells are killed by sodium butyrate. We have to find out how some of the remaining cancer cells can be killed or be converted to normal cells. Limited human studies suggest that sodium butyrate at high doses (up to 10 grams a day) is nontoxic and produces beneficial effects in some patients with advanced neuroblastomas and erythroid leukemia. However, many more experiments are needed before its usefulness for human cancer can be assessed.

Studies show that alpha-tocopheryl succinate enhances the antitumor effects of cAMP and sodium butyrate on neuroblastoma, glioma, and melanoma cells under laboratory conditions. The extent of alpha-tocopheryl succinate—induced enhancement depends upon the form of cancer and the type of agent. Thus, we are very encouraged to note that we now have at least six naturally occurring substances, namely beta-carotene; vitamins A, C, and E; cAMP; and butyric acid, that have been shown to produce anticancer effects on experimental systems and on certain types of advanced human cancer when used as a single agent. The combined effects of these agents on laboratory systems or on human cancer cells have not been evaluated.

Vitamin E enhances the beneficial effects of heat

During the last ten years extensive experiments and clinical studies of the effects of heat alone, or in combination with X-rays and certain chemicals, have been conducted. However, the results of clinical trials have been disappointing because the temperatures required to kill cancer cells are 42°–43°C and are fatal when the whole body is raised to these temperatures. Even in the treatment of local lesions, heat has been of very limited value; in addition, high temperatures (42°–43°C) increase the potential of X-rays to cause cancer. The use of heat in the treatment of tumors will continue to be restricted to local lesions until the cell-killing effects of heat can be achieved at temperatures near 40°C, which are not toxic to the whole body. Alpha-tocopheryl succinate in combination with heat at 40°C was more effective than the individual agents in reducing the growth of neuroblastoma cells *in vitro*. More animal and new human studies should be performed on the efficiency of the combined effect of alpha-tocopheryl succinate and heat in the management of cancer.

Vitamin C enhances or reduces the effects of chemotherapeutic agents and naturally occurring anticancer agents

Nontoxic concentrations of sodium ascorbate increase the growth inhibitory effect of several chemotherapeutic agents and some naturally occurring substances such as cAMP and sodium butyrate. Unlike vitamin E, sodium ascorbate reduces the killing effects of certain chemotherapeutic agents such as DTIC and methotrexate. These results suggest that whenever a combination of vitamin C and a chemotherapeutic agent is considered, it must be based on experimental results that support the desired effect. The addition of vitamin C without such a rationale may be ineffective or even counterproductive.

Vitamin C's ability to modify the effects of currently used tumor-therapeutic agents has not been tested adequately on either animal or human cancer. One study has shown, however, that sodium ascorbate combined with CCNU (a commonly used chemotherapeutic agent) enhances the survival of mice with leukemia twofold, in comparison with results obtained when CCNU is used alone. Further animal studies are needed before these findings can be applied to human cancer.

Beta-carotene and vitamins E, C , and D reduce the side effects of currently used chemotherapeutic agents

Beta-carotene appears to reduce the severity of radiation-induced mucositis (soreness of mouth) in humans. Vitamin E reduces doxorubicin-induced liver, heart, kidney, and intestine damage in animals. Alpha-tocopheryl succinate protects bone marrow against AZT-induced toxicity. Several animal studies have shown that vitamin E may reduce adriamycin-induced cardiac toxicity and skin ulcers. Vitamin E has also been shown to protect against bleomycin-induced lung fibrosis. Some studies have established that alpha-tocopheryl succinate is more effective than other forms of vitamin E in treating cancer. Reports show that vitamin E protects the immune system against the destructive effect of some chemotherapeutic agents, such as adriamycin, mitomycin C, and 5-fluorouracil. It has also been reported that sodium ascorbate significantly reduced adriamycin-induced heart damage in mice and guinea pigs. The relevance of these results to human beings is being tested. 1, 25 dihydroxy vitamin D_3 protects animals from chemotherapy-induced alopecia (baldness). Human trials should be performed to test the efficacy of these vitamins in reducing the adverse side effects of chemotherapeutic agents.

At this time these findings cannot be readily extrapolated to human cancer. Human studies are needed for confirmation. Available laboratory results suggest that adding beta-carotene and vitamins A, C, D, and E to currently used treatments may greatly improve their effectiveness. However, we must emphasize that the use of vitamins in combination with tumor-therapeutic agents must be done with a biological rationale; otherwise, the addition of vitamins may not be effective and may even be harmful. The role of other vitamins in combination with currently used tumor-therapeutic agents remains to be evaluated.

DESIGNING A NUTRITION AND LIFESTYLE PROGRAM FOR THOSE WHO ARE IN REMISSION AFTER BEING TREATED FOR CANCER

What is remission?
During remission, cancer cannot be detected by known technologies, either because there are very few cancer cells left or because there are no cancer cells at all.

How is remission achieved?
Surgery, extensive chemotherapy, and radiation therapy can produce a remission in certain types of tumors, if they are detected at early stages. These include neuroblastoma (a childhood tumor), Wilms' tumor (a kidney tumor), Hodgkin's disease (a tumor of blood cells), certain childhood leukemias (blood cancers), breast cancer, cervical cancer, prostate cancer, and melanoma (a type of skin cancer).

What are the consequences of classical cancer therapies?
There are four possible major consequences:

1. The person becomes free of cancer.

2. The original cancer may recur, generally within five to ten years, because a few cancer cells were left after treatment,

and they could not be eliminated by the body's defense system.

3. The person may be cured of the original cancer, but may develop new tumors ten to thirty years after treatment.

4. The person may develop noncancerous diseases such as paralysis, reproductive failure, increased aging, reduction in growth, aplastic anemia, cataract, and necrosis of several vital organs (brain, liver, muscle, etc.).

Some laboratory experiments suggest that we may be able to influence consequences 2, 3, and 4 above by designing an appropriate diet, together with appropriate amounts of supplemental beta-carotene; vitamins A, C, and E; and selenium. However, there are no human data yet to support these possibilities. An interim guideline is described below.

INTERIM DIET AND LIFESTYLE GUIDELINES

The recommendations are the same as described in the section, "Preventing Cancer." Reports show that a higher intake of total fat, saturated *and* polyunsaturated fatty acids, increases the chance of treatment failure in women with estrogen receptor-rich breast cancer who were in remission. Additional studies are needed to substantiate this. However, this does point out the value of a low-fat diet.

INTERIM SUPPLEMENTARY NUTRITION GUIDELINES

At this time there are no human data that permit the estimation of doses of vitamins and minerals that would be most effective in preventing or delaying the recurrence of cancer after remission has been achieved. Based on laboratory research, the following vitamin doses and dose schedules are suggested.

Beta-carotene

15 milligrams per day, taken orally.

Vitamin A (retinyl acetate)

5,000 I.U. per day, divided into two doses, taken orally, once in the morning and once in the evening.

Vitamin C

Up to 2 grams per day, taken orally, divided into at least two doses, in the form of calcium ascorbate.

Vitamin E

400 I.U. per day, divided into two doses, taken orally, once in the morning and once in the evening, each dose containing 100 I.U. of alpha-tocopheryl succinate and 100 I.U. of alpha-tocopherol.

B Vitamins

Limit the intake of B vitamins by taking a multiple vitamin that contains 2–5 times the RDA value, depending upon the type of B vitamins.

Selenium

100 micrograms per day, divided into two doses, taken orally, once in the morning and once in the evening. Selenium must be taken in the form of organic selenium. Inorganic selenium, such as sodium selenite, is absorbed poorly from the small intestine.

What results may be expected from such a program?

1. Prevention of cancer recurrence.

2. Marked delay of cancer recurrence.

3. Prevention or delay of onset of new cancer.

We must emphasize that the above suggestions regarding diet, supplemental vitamins, selenium, and lifestyle are based only on animal studies, some human studies, and the known safe limits of the nutrients.

Ongoing Clinical Trials with Nutrients and Aspirin

The contents of this table are based on a document obtained from the Chemoprevention Branch of the National Cancer Institute.

PRINCIPAL INVESTIGATOR ORGANIZATION	STUDY SITE POPULATION	AGENT– DOSAGE/SCHEDULE
Alberts, Davis, S., M.D. University of Arizona	Oral precancer	Beta-carotene Alpha-tocopherol Retinol
	Skin Basal cell Carcinoma of skin	Retinol–25,000 I.U./day 13-cis Retinoic acid– 0.15 mg/kg
	Colon Previous adenoma of colon	Wheat bran–13.5 or 2 g/day Calcium carbonate– 0.25 or 1.50 g/day
Balmes, James, E., M.D. University of California, San Francisco	Lung Heavy smokers	Beta-carotene– 30 mg/day Retinol–25,000 I.U./day

PRINCIPAL INVESTIGATOR ORGANIZATION	STUDY SITE POPULATION	AGENT– DOSAGE/SCHEDULE
Baron, John A., M.D., M.Sc. Dartmouth Medical School	Colon Previous colon polyp	Calcium carbonate– 1200 mg/day
	Colon Previous colon adenoma	Calcium carbonate– 1200 mg/day
	Colon Previous neo- plastic polyp	Aspirin–80 or 325 mg/day
Berman, Michael L., M.D. University of California, Irvine	Cervix Women with cervical displasia	Beta-carotene– 30 mg/day
Blackburn, George, L., M.D., Ph.D. New England Deaconess Hospital	Colon cancer	Omega-3 fatty acids–10 g/day
Bostick, Robert University of Minnesota (John D. Potter, M.D., Ph.D)	Colon High risk	Calcium carbonate– 3 or 5 g/day
Buring, Julie, E., D.Sc. Brigham & Women's Hospital	Lung Women smokers	Beta-carotene– 50 mg/day Vitamin E– 600 mg/day
Cullen, Mark R., M.D. Yale University	Lung	Beta-carotene– 50 mg/day Retinol–25,000 I.U./day
Goodman, Gary, M.D. University of Washington	Lung Cigarette smokers	Beta-carotene– 30 mg/day Retinol–25,000 I.U./day

PRINCIPAL INVESTIGATOR ORGANIZATION	STUDY SITE POPULATION	AGENT- DOSAGE/SCHEDULE
Greenberg, Robert E., M.D. Dartmouth College	Skin Basal cell carcinoma	Beta-carotene– 50 mg/day
	Colon Previous colon adenoma	Beta-carotene– 30 mg/day Ascorbic acid–1 g/day Alpha-tocopherol– 400 mg/day
Hennekens, Charles H., M.D. Harvard Medical School	All Physicians	Beta-carotene– 50 mg/day Aspirin–325 mg/day
Hong, Waun K., M.D. University of Texas	Head & neck Previous head & neck cancer, leukoplakia	13-cis Retinoic acid
	Lung Chronic smokers	13-cis Retinoic acid 1.0 mg/kg/day
	Oral cavity Oral leukoplakia	Beta-carotene 13-cis Retinoic acid
Keogh, James, P., M.D. University of Maryland	Lung	Beta-carotene– 30 mg/day Retinol–25.000 I.U./day
Luande, Gideon J., M.D. Tanzania Tumor Center	Skin cancer Albinos in Tanzania	Beta-carotene– 100 mg/day
Luk, Gordon, D., M.D. Dallas VA Medical Center	Colon Proliferation	Aspirin
McLarty, Jerry W., Ph.D. University of Texas	Lung Men exposed to asbestos daily	Retinol–25,000 I.U./day Beta-carotene– 50 mg/day
Meyskens, Frank L., M.D. University of Utah School of Medicine	Lung Heavy smokers	Beta-carotene– 30 mg/day

PRINCIPAL INVESTIGATOR ORGANIZATION	STUDY SITE POPULATION	AGENT– DOSAGE/SCHEDULE
Mobarhan, Sohrab, M.D. Loyola University of Chicago	Colon Previous colon	Beta-carotene– 30–180 mg/day
Omenn, Gilbert S., M.D., Ph.D. University of Washington	Lung Men with asbestosis	Beta-carotene– 30 mg/day Retinol–25,000 I.U./day
Romney, Seymour L., M.D. Albert Einstein College of Medicine	Cervix Women with cervical dysplasia	Beta-carotene– 30 mg/day
Surwit, Earl A., M.D. Southern Arizona Surgical	Cervix Women with mild/moderate dysplasia	Beta-trans retinoic acid–0.372%
Valanis, Barbara G., Ph.D. Kaiser Foundation Research Institute	Lung cancer	Beta-carotene– 30 mg/day Retinol–25,000 I.U./day

Major Studies on Vitamins, Nutrition, and Cancer

STUDIES ON CANCER TREATMENT

1. Dr. F. L. Meyskens Jr. (treatment of human cancer, vitamin A), University of California Cancer Center, Orange, CA 92668, U.S.

2. Dr. G. E. Goodman (treatment of human cancer, vitamin A), Tumor Institute of Swedish Hospital, Seattle, WA 98104, U.S.

3. Dr. G. Mathe (treatment of human cancer, vitamin A), Service des Maladies Sanguines et Tumorales, Institut de Cancérologie et d'Immunogénétique (INSERM U-50), Hopital, Paul-Brousse, F-94804, Fr.

4. Dr. G. J. S. Rustin (treatment of human cancer, vitamin A), Department of Medical Oncology, Charing Cross Hospital, London, W68 RF, U.K.

5. Dr. W. J. Uphouse (treatment of human cancer, vitamin A), Cancer Center of Hawaii, 1236 Lauhala Street, Rm 301, Honolulu, HI 96813, U.S.

6. Dr. L. Itri (treatment of human cancer, vitamin A), Hoffmann—La Roche, Inc., Nutley, NJ 07110, U.S.

7. Dr. N. J. Lowe (treatment of human cancer, vitamin A), Division of Dermatology, School of Medicine, University of California at Los Angeles, Los Angeles, CA 90024, U.S.

8. Dr. M. M. Black (treatment of human cancer, vitamins A and E), Department of Pathology, New York Medical College, Valhalla, NY 10595, U.S.

9. Dr. W. L. Robinson (treatment of human cancer, vitamin A), Division of Oncology, Department of Medicine, University of Colorado Health Sciences Center, Denver, CO 80262, U.S.

10. Dr. G. L. Peck (treatment of human cancer, vitamin A), Dermatology Branch, National Cancer Institute, Building 10, Bethesda, MD 20205, U.S.

11. Dr. W. Bollag and Dr. H. R. Hartmann (treatment of human cancer, vitamin A), Pharmaceutical Research Development, F. Hoffmann-La Roche & Co., Ltd., CH-4002, Basel, Switz.

12. Dr. L. Pauling (treatment of human cancer, vitamin C), 440 Page Mitt Road, Palo Alto, CA 94306, U.S.

13. Dr. F. Morishige (treatment of human cancer, vitamin C), Tachiarai Hospital, 842-1, Yamaguma Miwa-machi, Asakura-gun, Fukuoka, 838, Jpn.

14. Dr. A. Hanck (treatment of human cancer, vitamin C), Unit of Social and Preventive Medicine, University of Basel, Switz.

15. Dr. Vinod Kochupillai (human cancer, beta-carotene and vitamin E), All India Institutes of Medical Sciences, New Delhi, Ind.

16. Dr. R. T. Chlebowski (human cancer and vitamin K), School of Medicine, Harbor-UCLA Medical Center, Los Angeles, CA, U.S.

17. Dr. Abram Hoffer (human cancer and multiple vitamins), Hoffer Clinic, Victoria, British Columbia, Can.

18. Dr. Gian Maria Paganelli (vitamins), Istituto di Clinica Medica e Gastroenterologia, Policlinico S., Orsola, Via Massaranti 9, I-40138, Bologna, It.

19. Dr. Scott Lippman (beta-carotene retinoids), Department of Medical Oncology, University of Texas M.D. Anderson Cancer Center, Houston, TX 77030, U.S.

STUDIES ON HUMAN CANCER PREVENTION

20. Dr. T. Moon (vitamin A), Cancer Center, University of Arizona Health Sciences Center, Tucson, AZ 85724, U.S.

21. Dr. J. Li (vitamins A, C, and E), Department of Epidemiology and Cancer Institute, Chinese Academy of Medical Sciences, Beijing, People's Republic of China.

22. Dr. L. M. DeLuca, Dr. W. DeWys, Dr. P. Greenwald (vitamins A, C, and E), National Cancer Institute, Bethesda, MD 20205, U.S.

23. Dr. C. Hennekens (vitamin A), Harvard Medical School, Boston, MA 02115, U.S.

24. Dr. R. L. Phillips (diets), Loma Linda Studies School of Health, Loma Linda University, Loma Linda, CA 92350, U.S.

25. Dr. C. Mettlin (vitamin A), Roswell Park Memorial Institute, 666 Elm Street, Buffalo, NY 14263, U.S.

26. Dr. S. Graham (vitamin A), Departments of Sociology and Social and Preventive Medicine, State University of New York at Buffalo, Buffalo, NY 14214, U.S.

27. Dr. G. Kvale (vitamins A, C, and E), Institute of Hygiene and Social Medicine, University of Bergen, Nor.

28. Dr. M. Micksche (vitamin A), Institute of Cancer Research, University of Vienna, Ludwig Boltzmann Institute for Clinical Oncology, Municipal Hospital, Lainz-Vienna, Aus.

29. Dr. R. Doll (vitamins A, C, and E), Imperial Cancer Research Fund, Cancer Epidemiology Unit, 9 Keble Road, Oxford, OX13QG, U.K.

30. Dr. R. Peto (vitamins A, C, and E), Department of Clinical Medicine, Imperial Cancer Research Fund Cancer Unit, Nuffield, Radcliffe Infirmary, Oxford, OX26HE, U.K.

31. Dr. E. L. Wynder (diets), American Health Foundation, 320 East 43rd Street, New York, NY 10017, U.S.

32. Dr. J. Wylie-Rosett (vitamin A), Department of Community Health, Albert Einstein College of Medicine, 1300 Morris Park Avenue, Bronx, NY 10461, U.S.

33. Dr. A. J. Tuyns (vitamin C), Unit of Analytical Epidemiology, International Agency for Research on Cancer, 15–Cours Albert Thomas, F69372, Lyon, Cedex 08, Fr.

34. Dr. R. Burton (vitamins A, C, and E), Research Institute for Social Security, Helsinki, Fin.

35. Dr. P. Helms (vitamins A, C, and E), Institute of Hygiene, Aarhus, Den.

36. Dr. L. Bjerrum and Dr. A. Paerregaard (vitamins A, C, and E), St. Elizabeth Hospital, Copenhagen, Den.

37. Dr. J. H. Cummings and Dr. W. J. Branch (vitamins A, C, and E), Dunn Clinical Nutrition Center, Addenbrook's Hospital, Trumpington Street, Cambridge, U.K.

38. Dr. S. A. Broitman (alcohol and nutrition), Departments of Pathology and Microbiology, Boston University School of Medicine, Boston, MA 02118, U.S.

39. Dr. B. S. Reddy and Dr. J. H. Wisburger (fibers), Naylor Dana Institute for Disease Prevention, American Health Foundation, Valhalla, NY 10595, U.S.

40. Dr. T. Campbell (diets and nutrition), Division of Nutritional Sciences, Cornell University, Ithaca, NY 14850, U.S.

41. Dr. J. J. DeCosse (vitamins C and E), Department of Surgery, The New York Hospital Cornell Medical Center, 525 East 68th Street, New York, NY 10021, U.S.

42. Dr. G. A. Kune (nutrition and cancer), Department of Surgery, University of Melbourne, Richmond 3121, Victoria, Austral.

43. Dr. Shu-Yu (nutrition and cancer), Cancer Institute Chinese Academy of Medical Science, Beijing, Peoples Republic of China.

44. Dr. A. Costa (retinoids and cancer), Instituto Nazionale Tumori via Venezian 1, 20133 Milano, It.

45. Dr. Leonida Santamaria (beta-carotene and cancer), University of Pavia, Pavia, It.

46. Michael J. Hill (nutrition and cancer), PHLS-CAMR, Porton Down Salisbury, Wilts SP40JG, U.K.

47. Dr. G. H. McIntosh (nutrition and cancer), CS1R0 Division of Human Nutrition, Kintore Ave., Adelaide, S. Austral.

48. Dr. Paul Knekt, Social Insurance Institution, P.O. Box 78, SF-00381, Helsinki, Fin.

49. Dr. C. E. Butterworth (folate and vitamin B_{12}), Department of Nutrition Science, University of Alabama at Birmingham, Birmingham, AL 35294, U.S.

50. Dr. H. S. Garewal (retinoid and beta-carotene), Section of Hematology-Oncology, Tucson VA Medical Center, Tucson, AZ 85723, U.S.

51. Dr. Robert Bruce (vitamins), Ludwig Institute for Cancer Research, Toronto, Ontario, Can.

52. Dr. L. E. Holm (nutrition and cancer), Department of Cancer Prevention, Norrbacka, Karolinski Hospital, Stockholm, Swed.

53. Dr. E. C. Meyer (vitamin E), Department of Pharmacology, University of Pretoria, Pretoria, S. Afr.

54. Dr. E. B. Thorling, Danish Cancer Society, Department of Nutrition and Cancer, Norrebrograle 44 DK-8000, Den.

55. Dr. N. V. Zandwick, The Netherlands Cancer Institute, Plesmanlaan 121, 1066 CX Amsterdam, Neth.

LABORATORY STUDIES

56. Dr. E. Seifter (vitamin A), Department of Surgery, Albert Einstein College of Medicine, 1300 Morris Park Avenue, Bronx, NY 10461, U.S.

57. Dr. R. C. Moon (vitamin A), Laboratory of Pathophysiology, Life Sciences Building, IIT Research Institute, Chicago, IL 60616, U.S.

58. Dr. T. K. Basu (vitamins A and C), Department of Food and Nutrition, University of Alberta, Edmonton, Alberta, T6G2M8, Can.

59. Dr. L. Santamaria (vitamin A), C. Golgi Institute of General Pathology, University of Pavia, Piazza Botta n. 10, I-27100 Pavia, It.

60. Dr. R. W. Shearer (vitamin A), 2017 East Beaver Lake Drive, Issaquah, WA 98027, U.S.

61. Dr. N. T. Telang (vitamins), Laboratory of Molecular Biology and Virology, Memorial Sloan-Kettering Cancer Center, New York, NY 10021, U.S.

62. Dr. S. Takase (vitamins), Departments of Nutrition and Biochemistry, Shizuoka Women's University, 409 Yada, Shizuoka-City, Shizuoka 422, Jpn.

63. Dr. T. J. Slaga (vitamins A, C, and E), The University of Texas System Cancer Center, Science Park-Research Division, Smithville, TX 78957, U.S.

64. Dr. P Newberne (vitamin E and selenium), Massachusetts Institute of Technology, 50 Ames Street, Cambridge, MA 02139, U.S.

65. Dr. K. N. Prasad (vitamins E and C), Department of Radiology, Center for Vitamin and Cancer Research, University of Colorado Health Sciences Center, Denver, CO 80262, U.S.

66. Dr. E. Bright-See (vitamins E and C) and Dr. H. Newmark (vitamins), Ludwig Institute for Cancer Research, 9 Earl Street, Toronto, Ontario, M4YlM4, Can.

67. Dr. R. P. Tengerdy (vitamin E), Department of Microbiology, Colorado State University, Fort Collins, CO 80523, U.S.

68. Dr. S. V. Kandarkar (vitamin A), Cancer Research Institute, Parel Bombay, Ind.

69. Dr. D. G. Hendricks (vitamins), Departments of Nutrition and Food Sciences, Utah State University, Logan, UT 84322, U.S.

70. Dr. R. Lotan (vitamin A), Department of Tumor Biology, M. D. Anderson Hospital and Tumor Institute, Houston, TX 77030, U.S.

71. Dr. Y. M. Yang (vitamin E), M. D. Anderson Hospital and Tumor Institute, University of Texas System Cancer Center, Houston, TX 77030, U.S.

72. Dr. L. W. Wattenberg (vitamin E and other antioxidants), Department of Pathology, University of Minnesota, Minneapolis, MN 55455, U.S.

73. Dr. B. P. Sani (vitamin C), Kettering Meyer Laboratory, Southern Research Institute, Birmingham, AL 35203, U.S.

74. Dr. A. M. Jetten (vitamin A), National Institute of Environmental Health Sciences, Research Triangle, NC 27709, U.S.

75. Dr. E. P. Norkus (vitamin C), Dr. H. Bhagavan (vitamins A, C, and E), and Dr. L. Machlin (vitamin E), Hoffmann-La Roche, Inc., Nutley, NJ 07110, U.S.

76. Dr. R. Gol-Winkler (vitamin C), Laboratoire de Chimie Médicale, Institut de Pathlogie, Université de Liège, Bâtiment B-23, B-4000, Start Tilman Par Liège 1, Belg.

77. Dr. C. H. Park (vitamin C), Department of Medicine, University of Kansas Medical Center, Kansas City, KS 66103, U.0.

78. Dr. V. P. Sethi (vitamin C), Oncology Research Center, Bowman Gray School of Medicine of Wake Forest University, Winston-Salem, NC 27103, U.S.

79. Dr. J. A. Eisman (vitamins), University of Melbourne, Respiratory General Hospital, Heidelberg 3084, Victoria, Austral.

80. Dr. M. Hozumi (vitamins A and E), Department of Chemotherapy, Saitama Cancer Center, Research Unit, Saitama—362, Jpn.

81. Dr. L. H. Chen (vitamins C and E), Departments of Nutrition and Food Sciences, University of Kentucky, Lexington, KY 40506, U.S.

82. Dr. H. Fortmeyer (vitamins), Tieversuchsanlage des Klinikum der J. W. Goeth-universitat, Theodor Stern Ka 17, D-6000, Frankfurt, W. Ger.

83. Dr. M. B. Sporn (vitamin A), Laboratory of Chemoprevention, National Cancer Institute, Bethesda, MD 20892, U.S.

84. Dr. F. Chytil (vitamin A), Departments of Biochemistry and Medicine, Vanderbilt University, School of Medicine, Nashville, TN 37240, U.S.

85. Dr. A. T. Diplock (vitamin E and selenium), Department of Biochemistry, Royal Free Hospital, School of Medicine, University of London, London, U.K.

86. Dr. A. Trichopoulou (vitamins), Departments of Nutrition and Biochemistry, Athens School of Hygiene, Leof Alexandria 196, GR-11521, Athens, Gr.

87. Dr. G. N. Schrauzer (selenium), Department of Chemistry, University of California at San Diego, La Jolla, CA 92093, U.S.

88. Dr. J. W. Thanassi (vitamin B_{12}), Department of Biochemistry, University of Vermont, College of Medicine, Burlington, VT 05405, U.S.

89. Dr. G. P. Tryfiates (vitamin B_{12}), Department of Biochemistry, West Virginia University, School of Medicine, Morgantown, WV 26506, U.S.

90. Dr. D. G. Zaridze (vitamins), WHO, Centre International de Recherche sur le Cancer, 150 cours Albert-Thomas 69732, Lyon, Cedex 08, Fr.

91. Dr. M. H. Zile (vitamins), Departments of Food Sciences and Human Nutrition, Michigan State University, East Lansing, MI 48824, U.S.

92. Dr. H. Fujuki (vitamins) and Dr. T. Sugimura (vitamins), National Cancer Center Research Institute, 1-1, Tsukijil, 5-Chome, Chou-ku, Tokyo, 104, Jpn.

93. Dr. A. E. Rogers (vitamins), Departments of Nutrition and Food Sciences, Massachusetts Institute of Technology, Cambridge, MA 02139, U.S.

94. Dr. T. R. Breitmann (vitamins), National Cancer Institute, Bethesda, MD 20205, U.S.

95. Dr. P. B. McCay (vitamin E and antioxidants), Oklahoma Medical Foundation, Oklahoma City, OK 73104, U.S.

96. Dr. J. C. Bertram (vitamins), Grace Cancer Drug Center, Roswell Park Memorial Institute, 666 Elm Street, Buffalo, NY 14263, U.S.

97. Dr. F. E. Jones (vitamin A), Department of Surgery, College of Medicine, 8700 West Wisconsin Avenue, Milwaukee, WI 53226, U.S.

98. Dr. B. S. Alam (vitamin A), Department of Biochemistry, Louisiana State University Medical Center, New Orleans, LA 70119, U.S.

99. Dr. G. Shklar (vitamin E), Departments of Oral Medicine and Oral Pathology, Harvard School of Dental Medicine, Boston, MA 02115, U.S.

100. Dr. D. M. Klurfeld (vitamin A), The Wistar Institute of Anatomy and Biology, 36th Street at Spruce, Philadelphia, PA 19104, U.S.

101. Dr. S. J. Van Rensburg (vitamin A), National Research Institute for Nutritional Diseases, Tygerberg, 7505, S. Afr.

102. Dr. D. M. Disorbo (vitamin B_6), Oncology Research Laboratory, Nassau Hospital, Mineola, NY 11501, U.S.

103. Dr. Y. Tomita (vitamin A), Department of Public Health, Kurume University School of Medicine, Kurume-830, Jpn.

104. Dr. A. R. Kennedy (protease inhibitors and antioxidants), Department of Radiation Oncology, University of Pennsylvania Medical School, 3400 Spruce Street, Philadelphia, PA 19104, U.S.

105. Dr. K. K. Carroll (fat), Department of Biochemistry, University of Western Ontario, London, Ontario, N6A5C1, Can.

106. Dr. B. N. Ames (diets and vitamins), Department of Biochemistry, University of California, Berkeley, CA 94720, U.S.

107. Dr. I. Emerit (antioxidants), Université de Pierre et Marie Curie, Paris, Fr.

108. Dr. D. Schmahl (vitamin C), Institute of Toxicology and Chemotherapy, German Cancer Research Center, Heidelberg, W. Ger.

109. Dr. Y. S. Hong (vitamins A, C, and E), Ewha Women's University, College of Medicine, Seoul, S. Ko.

110. Dr. C. Ip (vitamin E and selenium), Department of Breast Surgery, Roswell Park Memorial Institute, Buffalo, NY 14263, U.S.

111. Dr. L. G. Israels (vitamin K), Manitoba Institute of Cell Biology, University of Manitoba, Winnipeg, Manitoba, Can.

112. Dr. R. G. Ham (nutrients), Department of Molecular, Cellular, and Developmental Biology, University of Colorado, Boulder, CO 80309, U.S.

113. Dr. J. P. Berry (selenium), SC 27 Inserm, Laboratoire de Biophysique, Faculté de Médecine, 94010, Créteil, Fr.

114. Dr. M. Sakaguchi (fat), Department of Surgery, Kansai Medical University, 1 Fumizono, Moriguchi, Osaka, 570, Jpn.

115. Dr. S. M. Przybyszewski (vitamin E and other antioxidants), Department of Biochemistry, Institute of Hematology, 00-957, Warsaw, Pol.

116. Dr. C. Beckman (vitamin E), Biology Department, Concordia University, Montreal, Quebec, Can.

117. Dr. M. Menkes and Dr. G. Comstock (vitamin E), The Johns Hopkins Training Center for Public Health Research, Hagerstown, MD 21740, U.S.

118. Dr. J. T. Salomen (selenium and human cancer), Department of Community Health, Research Institute of Public Health, University of Kuopio, 70211 Kuopio-1, Fin.

119. Dr. M. G. Le (alcohol and human cancer), Institute Gustave Roussy, Villejuif, Fr.

120. Dr. J. A. Milner (selenium and animal cancer), Department of Food Science, Division of Nutritional Sciences, University of Illinois, Urbana, IL 61801, U.S.

121. Dr. A. A. Yunis (vitamin D), Department of Medicine, University of Miami School of Medicine, Miami, FL 033101, U.S.

122. Dr. M. Murakoshi (carotenoids), Oleochemistry Research Center Lion Corporation, 7-13-12 Hirai, Edogawa-Ku, Tokyo 132, Jpn.

123. Dr. H. Takada (vitamin E), Department of Surgery, Kansai Medical University, Moriguchi, Osaka 570, Jpn.

124. Dr. K. Kline (vitamin E), Division of Nutritional Sciences, GEA 117, University of Texas, Austin, TX 78712-1097, U.S.

125. Dr. W. A. Behrens (vitamin E), Bureau of Nutritional Sciences Food Directorate, Health Protection Branch, Health and Welfare, Tunney's Pasture, Ottawa, Ontario, Can.

126. Dr. Clinton J. Grubbs (vitamin A), Department of Nutrition Sciences, University of Alabama at Birmingham, Birmingham, AL 35294, U.S.

127. Dr. A. Verma (retinoids), University of Wisconsin Clinical Cancer Center, Madison, WI 53792, U.S.

128. Dr. Maryce M. Jacobs (nutrition and cancer), American Institute for Cancer Research, 1759 R Street, N.W., Washington DC 20009, U.S.

129. Dr. J. L. Schwartz (vitamins A and E), Harvard School of Dental Medicine, Dana Farber Cancer Institute, Boston, MA, U.S.

Further Reading

Ames, B. N. Dietary carcinogens and anticarcinogens. *Science.* 221: 1256–64, 1983.

Barone, J., Taioli, E., Hebert, J. R., et al. Vitamin supplement use and risk of oral and esophageal cancer. *Nutrition and Cancer.* 18: 31–41, 1992.

Behrens, W. A., and Madère, R. Tissue discrimination between RRR-a- and all-rac-a-tocopherols in rats. *Journal of Nutrition.* 121: 454–59, 1991.

Bendich, A., and Olson, J. A. Biological actions of carotenoids, *The Federation of American Society for Experimental Biology Journal.* 3: 1927–32, 1989.

Benedict, W. F., Wheatley, W. L., and Jones, P. A. Inhibition of chemically induced morphological transformation and reversion of the transformed phenotype by ascorbic acid in $C_3H/10T\frac{1}{2}$ cells. *Cancer Research.* 40: 2796–2801, 1980.

Bianchi-Santamaria, A., Fedeli, S., and Santamaria, L. Possible activity of beta-carotene in patients with the AIDS-related complex, a pilot study. *Medical Oncology and Tumor Pharmatherapeutics.* 9: 151–53, 1992.

Bjelke, E. Dietary vitamin A and human lung cancer. *International Journal of Cancer.* 15: 562–65, 1975.

Black, M. M., Zachrau, R. E., Dion, A. S., et al. Stimulation of prognostically favorable cell-mediated immunity of breast cancer patients by high dose vitamin A and vitamin E. In: *Vitamins, Nutrition and Cancer.* Edited by K. N. Prasad, 134–46. Basel: Karger Press, 1984.

Blot, J., Li, J-Y., Taylor, P. R., et al. Nutrition intervention trials in Linxian, China: supplementation with specific vitamins/mineral combinations, cancer incidence, and disease-specific mortality in the general population. *Journal of the National Cancer Institute.* 85: 1483–92, 1993.

Boutwell, R. K. Biology and biochemistry of the two-step model of carcinogenesis. In: *Modulation and Mediation of Cancer by Vitamins.* Edited by F. L. Meyskens, Jr., and K. N. Prasad, 2–9. Basel: Karger Press, 1983.

Broitman, S. A. Relationship of ethanolic beverages and ethanol to cancers of the digestive tract. *Vitamins, Nutrition and Cancer.* Edited by K. N. Prasad, 195–211. Basel: Karger Press, 1984.

Cameron, E., and Pauling, L. *Vitamin C and Cancer.* New York: Warner Books, 1981.

Carini, R., Poli, G., Dianzani, M. V., et al. Comparative evaluation of the antioxidant activity of a-tocopherol, a- tocopherol polyethylene glycol 1000 succinate and a-tocopheryl succinate in isolated hepatocytes and liver microsomal suspensions. *Biochemical Pharmacology.* 39: 1597–1601, 1990.

Chow, C. K., Thacker, R. R., Changchit, C., et al. Lower levels of vitamin C and carotenes in plasma of cigarette smokers. *Journal of the American College of Nutrition.* 5: 305–12, 1986.

Cohrs, R. J., Torelli, S., Prasad, K. N., et al. Effect of vitamin E succinate and cAMP-stimulating agent on the expressions of c-*myc*, N-*myc* and H-*ras* in murine neuroblastoma cells. *International Journal of Developmental Neuroscience.* 9: 187–94, 1991.

Cook, M. G., and McNamara, P. Effect of dietary vitamin E on dimethylhydrazine-induced colonic tumor in mice. *Cancer Research.* 40: 1329–31, 1980.

DeCosse, J. J., Miller, H. H., and Lesser, M. L. Effect of wheat fiber and vitamins C and E on rectal polyps in patients with familial adenomatous polyposis. *Journal of the National Cancer Institute.* 81: 1290–97, 1989.

Diet, Nutrition and Cancer, National Academy of Sciences Press: Washington, DC, 1982.

Disorbo, D. M., and Nathanson, L. High dose pyridoxal supplemented culture medium inhibits the growth of a human malignant melanoma cell line. *Nutrition and Cancer.* 5: 10–15, 1983.

Doll, R., and Peto, R. The cause of cancer. Quantitative estimates of available risks of cancer in the United States today. *Journal of the National Cancer Institute.* 66: 1192–1308, 1981.

Duthie, G. G., and Arthur, J. R. Vitamin E supplementation of smokers and non-smokers. *Fat Science and Technology.* 11: 456–58, 1990.

Flavin, D. F., and Kolbye, A. C., Jr. Nutritional factors with a potential to inhibit critical pathways of tumor promotion. In: *Modulation and Mediation of Cancer by Vitamins.* Edited by F. L. Meyskens, Jr., and K. N. Prasad, 24–38. Basel: Karger Press, 1983.

Fryburg, D. A., Mark, R., Askenase, P. V., et al. The immunostimulatory effects and safety of beta-carotene in patients with AIDS. VIII International Conference on AIDS/

III STD, World Congress, POB3458, B163, Amsterdam, 1992.

Garewal, H. S., and Meyskens, F. L., Jr. Retinoids and carotenoids in the prevention of oral cancer: a critical appraisal. *Cancer Epidemiology, Biomarkers and Prevention*. 1: 155–59, 1992.

Geetha, A., Sankar, R., Mara, T., et al. A-tocopherol reduces doxorubicin-induced toxicity in rats — histological and biochemical evidence. *Indian Journal of Physiology and Pharmacology*. 34: 94–100, 1990.

Gogn, S. R., Lertora, J. L., George, W. J., et al. Protection of Zidovudine-induced toxicity against murine eythroid progenitor cells by vitamin E. *Experimental Hematology*. 19: 649–52, 1991.

Graham, S., Mettlin, C., Marshall, J., et al. Dietary factors in the epidemiology of cancer of the larnyx. *American Journal of Epidemiology*. 113: 675–80, 1981.

Griffin, A. C. Role of selenium in the chemoprevention of cancer. *Advances in Cancer Research*. 29: 419–42, 1979.

Haffke, S. C., and Seeds, N. W. Neuroblastoma: The *E. coli* of neurobiology. *Life Sciences*. 16: 1649–58, 1975.

Hazuka, M. B., Edwards-Prasad, J., Newman, F., et al. Beta-carotene induces morphological differentiation and decreases adenylate cyclase activity in melanoma cells in culture. *Journal of the American College of Nutrition*. 9: 143–44, 1990.

Heimburger. D. C., Alexander, B., Birch, R., et al. Improvement in bronchial squamous metaplasia in smokers treated with folate and vitamin B_{12}. *Journal of the American Medical Association*. 259: 1525–30, 1988.

Higginson, J., and Muir, C. S. Environmental carcinogenesis: Misconceptions and limitations to cancer control. *Journal of the National Cancer Institute*. 63: 1291–98, 1979.

Holm, L. E., Nordevang, E., Hjalmar, M. L., et al. Treatment failure and dietary habits in women with breast cancer. *Journal of the National Cancer Institute*. 85: 32–36, 1993.

Hong, W. K., Lippman, S. M., Itri, L. M., et al. Prevention of second primary tumors with isotretinoin in squamous-cell carcinoma of the head and neck. *New England Journal of Medicine*. 323: 795–801, 1990.

Imashuku, S., Sugano, T., Fukiwara, K., et al. Intra-aortic prostaglandin E1 (PGE1) infusion, papaverine and multiagent chemotherapy in disseminated neuroblastoma. *Cancer Research*. 23: 478a, 1983.

Imashuku, S., Todo, S., Amano, T., et al. Cyclic AMP in neuroblastoma, ganglioneuroma, and sympathetic ganglia. *Experientia*. 33: 1507, 1977.

Ingold, K. U., Burton, G. W., Foster, D. O., et al. Biokinetics of and discrimination between dietary RRR- and SRR-a-tocopherols in the male rat. *Lipids*. 22: 163–72, 1987.

Jain, M., Cook, G. M., Davis, F. G., et al. A case control study of diet and colorectal cancer. *International Journal of Cancer*. 26: 757–68, 1980.

Jimenez, J. J., and Yunis, A. A. Protection from chemotherapy-induced alopecia by 1, 25-dihydroxy Vitamin D_3. *Cancer Research*. 52: 5123–25, 1992.

Jones, F. E., Komorowski, R. A., and Condon, R. E. The effects of ascorbic acid and butylated hydroxyanisole in the chemoprevention of 1, 2-dimethylhydrazine-induced large bowel neoplasm. *Journal of Surgical Oncology*. 25: 54–60, 1984.

Kennedy, A. R. Prevention of radiation transformation in-vitro. In: *Vitamins, Nutrition and Cancer*. Edited by K. N. Prasad, 166–79. Basel: Karger Press, 1984.

Khan, M. A., Jenkins, K. G., Tolleson, W. H., et al. Retinoic acid inhibition of human papilloma virus type 16-mediated transformation of human keratinocytes. *Cancer Research.* 53: 905–9, 1993.

Kinlen, L. J., and McPherson, K. Pancreas cancer and coffee and tea consumption. A case-control study. *British Journal of Cancer.* 49: 93–96, 1984.

Klurfeld, D. M., Aglow, E., Tepper, S. A., et al. Modification of dimethyl-hydrazine-induced carcinogenesis in rats by dietary cholesterol. *Nutrition and Cancer.* 5: 16–23, 1983.

Knekt, P. Role of vitamin E in the prophylaxis of cancer. *Annals of Medicine.* 23: 3–12, 1991.

Kritchevsky, D. Diet and nutrition research. *Cancer.* 62: 1839–43, 1988.

Kummet, T., Moon, T. E., and Meyskens, F. L., Jr. Vitamin A: Evidence for its preventive role in human cancer. *Nutrition and Cancer.* 5: 96–106, 1983.

Kune, G. A., and Vitetta, L. Alcohol consumption and the etiology of colorectal cancer: A review of scientific evidence from 1957 to 1991. *Nutrition and Cancer.* 18: 97–111, 1992.

Kurek, M. P., and Corwin, L. M. Vitamin E protection against tumor formation by transplanted murine sarcoma cells. *Nutrition and Cancer.* 4: 128–39, 1982.

Lambooy, J. P. Influence of riboflavin antagonists on azodye hepatoma induction in the rat. *Proceedings of the Society for Experimental Biology and Medicine.* 153: 532–35, 1976.

Lapré, J. A., De Vries, H. T., Koeman, J. H., et al. The antiproliferative effect of dietary calcium on colonic epithelium is mediated by luminal surfactants and dependent on the type of dietary fat. *Cancer Research.* 53: 784–89, 1993.

Le, M.G., Hill, C., Kramar, A., et al. Alcoholic beverage consumption and breast cancer in a French case-control study. *American Journal of Epidemiology.* 120: 350–57, 1984.

Lippman, S. M., and Meyskens, F. L., Jr. Vitamin A derivatives in the prevention and treatment of human cancer. *Journal of the American College of Nutrition.* 7: 269–84, 1988.

Lotan, R. Effect of vitamin A and its analogs (retinoids) on normal and neoplastic cells. *Biophysica Acta.* 605: 33–91, 1981.

Menkes, M., and Constock, G. Vitamin A and E and lung cancer. *American Journal of Epidemiology.* 120: 491 (abstract), 1984.

Meyskens, F. L., Jr. Prevention and treatment of cancer with vitamin A and retinoids. In: *Vitamins, Nutrition and Cancer.* Edited by K. N. Prasad, 266–73. Basel: Karger Press, 1984.

Meyskens, F. L., Jr. and Prasad, K. N. eds. *Modulation and Mediation of Cancer by Vitamins,* 1–348. Basel: Karger Press, 1983.

Mihich, E., Rosen, F. and Nichol, C. A. The effect of pyridoxine deficiency on a spectrum of mouse and rat tumors. *Cancer Research.* 19: 1244–48, 1959.

Murakoshi, M., Nishino, H., Satomi, Y., et al. Potent prevention action of a-carotene against carcinogenesis: Spontaneous liver carcinogenesis and promoting stage of lung and skin carcinogenesis in mice are suppressed more effectively by carotene than by B-carotene. *Cancer Research.* 52: 6583–87, 1992.

Newbern, P. M., and Suphakarn, V. Nutrition and cancer. A review with emphasis on the role of vitamin C, vitamin E and selenium. *Nutrition and Cancer.* 5: 107–17, 1983.

Newmark, H. L., and Lipkin, M. Colonic hyperplasia and hyperproliferation induced in rodents by a nutritional stress diet containing 4 factors of the Western human diet: high fat and phosphate, low calcium and vitamin D. In: *Calcium, Vitamin D and Prevention of Colon Cancer,* M. Lipkin, H. L. Newmark, and G. Kelloff, eds., 145–54, Boca Raton, FL: CRC Press, Inc., 1991.

Novogrodsky, A., Dvir, A., Sholnik, T., et al. Effect of polar organic compounds on leukemic cells: Butyrate induced partial remission of acute myelogenous leukemia in a child. *Cancer.* 51: 9–11, 1983.

Odukoya, O., Hawach, F., and Shaklar, G. Retardation of experimental oral cancer by topical vitamin E. *Nutrition and Cancer.* 6: 98–104, 1984.

Ohkoshi, M., Ohta, H., and Ito, M. Effect of vitamin B_2 on tumorigenesis of 3-methylcholanthrene in the mouse. *Gann* (Jpn). 73: 105–7, 1982.

Paganelli, G. M., Biasco, G., Brandi, G., et al. Effect of vitamins A, C, and E supplementation on rectal cell proliferation in patients with colorectal adenomas. *Journal of the National Cancer Institute.* 84: 47–51, 1992.

Palgi, A. Vitamin A and lung cancer. *Nutrition and Cancer.* 6: 105–19, 1984.

Prasad, K. N. Butyric acid: a small fatty acid with diverse biological functions. *Life Sciences.* 27: 1351–58, 1980.

———. Differentiation of neuroblastoma cells in culture. *Biological Reviews.* 50: 129–65, 1975.

———. ed. *Vitamins, Nutrition and Cancer,* 1–400, Basel: Karger Press, 1984.

———. Induction of differentiated phenotypes in melanoma cells by a combination of an adenosine 3, 5, -cyclic monophosphate stimulating agent and d-alpha-tocopheryl succinate. *Cancer Letters.* 44: 17–22, 1989.

———. Therapeutic potentials of differentiating agents in neuroblastomas. *Biology of Cancer* (2). Edited by E. A. Mirand, W. B. Hutchinson, and E. Mihich, 75–89. New York: Alan R. Liss, 1983.

Prasad, K. N., Cohrs, R. J., and Sharma, O. K. Decreased expression of c-*myc* and H-*ras* oncogenes in vitamin E succinate-induced morphologically differentiated murine B-16 melanoma cells in culture. *Biochemistry and Cell Biology.* 68: 1250–55, 1990.

Prasad, K. N, and Edwards-Prasad, J. Effect of tocopherol (vitamin E) acid succinate on morphological alteration and growth inhibition in melanoma cells in culture. *Cancer Research.* 43: 550–55, 1982.

———. Vitamin E and cancer prevention. Recent advances and future potentials. *Journal of the American College of Nutrition.* 11: 487–500, 1992.

Prasad, K. N., and Meyskens, F. L., Jr., eds. *Nutrients and Cancer Prevention,* New Jersey: Humana Press, 1990.

Prasad, K. N., and Rama, B. N. Modification of the effect of pharmacological agents on tumor cells in culture by vitamin C and vitamin E. In: *Modulation and Mediation of Cancer by Vitamins.* Edited by F. L. Meyskens Jr., and K. N. Prasad, 244–57. Basel: Karger Press, 1983.

Recommended Dietary Allowances, 9th Edition, National Academy of Sciences, Washington, DC, 1980.

Recommended Dietary Allowances, 10th Edition, National Academy of Sciences, Washington, DC, 1989.

Reddy, B. S. Dietary macronutrients and colon cancer. In: *Vitamins Nutrition and Cancer.* Edited by K. N., Prasad, 212–30. Basel: Karger Press, 1984.

Rimm, E. B., Stampfer, M. J., Ascherio, A., et al. Vitamin E consumption and the risk of coronary disease in men. *New England Journal of Medicine.* 328: 1450–56, 1993.

Risch, H. A., Howe, G. R., Jain M., et al. Are female smokers at higher risk for lung cancer than male smokers?: A case-control analysis by histologic type. *American Journal of Epidemiology.* 138: 281–93, 1993.

Rosenberg, R. N. Neuroblastoma and glioma cell cultures in studies of neurologic functions: The clinician's Rosetta Stone. *Neurology.* 27: 105–8, 1977.

Sahu, S. N., Edwards-Prasad, J., and Prasad, K. N. Effect of alpha-tocopheryl succinate on adenylate cyclase activity in murine neuroblastoma cells in culture. *Journal of the American College of Nutrition.* 7: 285–93, 1988.

Salonen, J. T., Alfthan, G., Huttunen, J. K., et al. Association between serum selenium and the risk of cancer. *American Journal of Epidemiology.* 120: 342–49, 1984.

Schrauzer, G. N. Selenium in nutritional cancer prophylaxis: An update. In: *Vitamins, Nutrition and Cancer.* Edited by K. N. Prasad, 240–50. Basel: Karger Press, 1984.

Shamberger, R. J., Baughman, F. F., Kalchert, S. L., et al. Carcinogen-induced chromosomal breakage decreased by antioxidants. *Proceedings of National Academy of Sciences.* 70: 1461–63, 1973.

Shklar, G., Schwartz, J., Trickler, D. et al. Regression of experimental cancer by oral administration of combined d-tocopherol and beta-carotene. *Nutrition and Cancer.* 12: 321–25, 1989.

Slaga, T. J. Multistage skin carcinogenesis and specificity of inhibitors. In: *Modulation and Mediation of Cancer by Vitamins.* Edited by F. L. Meyskens Jr., and K. N. Prasad, 10–23. Basel: Karger Press, 1983.

Sporn, M. B. Retinoids and carcinogenesis. *Nutritional Reviews.* 35: 65–69, 1977.

Sporn, M. B., Roberts, A. B., and Goodman, D. S., eds. *The Retinoids.* Orlando: Academic Press, 1984.

Sram, R. J., Samkova, I., and Hola, N. High dose ascorbic acid prophylaxis in workers occupationally exposed to halogenated ethers. *Journal of Hygiene, Epidemiology, Microbiology, and Immunology.* 27: 305–18, 1983.

Stampfer, M. J., Hennekens, C. H., Manson, J. E., et al. Vitamin E consumption and the risk of coronary disease in women. *New England Journal of Medicine.* 328: 1444–49, 1993.

Stich, H. F., Rosin, M. P., Horby, A. P., et al. Remission of oral leukoplakias and micronuclei in tobacco/betel quid chewers treated with beta-carotene and with beta-carotene plus vitamin A. *International Journal of Cancer.* 42: 195–99, 1988.

Sugiyama, M., Lin, X., and Costa, M. Protective effect of vitamin E against chromosomal aberrations and mutation induced by sodium chromate in Chinese hamster ovary V-19 cells. *Mutation Research.* 260: 19–23, 1991.

Tannebaum, S. R., and Wishnok, J. S. Inhibition of nitrosamine formation by ascorbic acid. *Annals of New York Academy of Sciences.* 498: 354–63, 1987.

Tryfiates, G. P. Control of tumor growth by pyridoxine restriction or treatment with an antivitamin agent. *Cancer Detection and Prevention.* 4: 159–64, 1981.

Tryfiates, G. P., and Prasad, K. N. eds. *Nutrition, Growth and Cancer.* New York: Alan R. Liss, 1988.

Turley, J. M., Sander, B. G., and Kline, K. RRR-a-tocopheryl succinate modulation of human promyelocytic leukemia (HL-60) cell proliferation and differentiation. *Nutrition and Cancer.* 18: 201–13, 1992.

Tuyns, A. J. Alcohol and cancer. *Proceedings of the Nutrition Society.* 49: 145–51, 1990.

Wald, N. J., Boreham, J., and Hayward, J. L. Plasma retinol, beta-carotene and vitamin E levels in relation to the future risk of breast cancer. Prospective studies involving 5,000 women. *British Journal of Cancer.* 49: 321–24, 1984.

Wylie-Rosett, J., Romney, S., Slagle, S., et al. Influence of vitamin A on cervical dysplasia and carcinoma in-situ. *Nutrition and Cancer.* 6: 49–57, 1984.

Wynder, E. L., and Gori, G. B. Contribution of the environment to cancer incidence: An epidemiologic exercise. *Journal of the National Cancer Institute.* 58: 825–32, 1977.

Yasunaga, et al. Protective effect of vitamin E against immunosuppression induced by adriamycin, mitomycin C, and 5-fuorouracil in mice. *Nippon Geka Hokan* (Jpn). 52: 591–601, 1983.

Youngman, L. D., and Campbell, T. C. The sustained development of preneoplastic lesions depends on high protein intake. *Nutrition and Cancer.* 18: 131–42, 1992.

Zedek, M.S., and Lipkin, M. eds. *Inhibition of tumor induction and development.* New York: Plenum Press, 1981.

Index

111

In response to increasing demands from readers, Dr. Prasad has developed vitamin products based on the most recent scientific studies. Detailed information about these products can be obtained from:

Scientific Nutrition, Inc.
351 Fairfax Street
Denver, CO 80220
1-800-796-4640
Fax: 303-394-2642